"You didn't want me to feel that I had to stay."

It really wasn't fair. The man was always a couple of steps ahead of her. He came closer. So gently, he cradled her face between his hands. Gabe's palms were warm against her cheeks and he smelled of some light, tempting aftershave. "Well, I *want* to stay."

Mary wrapped her fingers around his wrists. At her slight tug, his hands dropped away. And something scary happened within her—a sadness, a longing. She wished that he would touch her again, deliberately, the way he'd just done. Tenderly. The way a man will touch a wife.

Or a lover…

Dear Reader,

Welcome to a whole new branch of the Bravo family.

In the coming months, Special Edition will be bringing you the stories of the children of Davis and Aleta Bravo. Some of you may have read the first installment, *The Stranger and Tessa Jones,* this past January.

This month, the saga continues with *The Bravo Bachelor,* in which smooth-talking confirmed bachelor Gabe Bravo meets more than his match in down-to-earth widow Mary Hofstetter. He's been sent to buy her land, and Gabe always gets what he's after. But the eight-and-a-half months pregnant Mary is one determined woman. She loves the ranch her husband left her and she will never sell.

Watch for more of this proud Texas dynasty coming up in June and December. Davis and Aleta had seven sons and two daughters, so I've got a whole bunch of new stories to tell.

Happy reading, everyone!

Yours always,

Christine Rimmer

CHRISTINE RIMMER

THE BRAVO BACHELOR

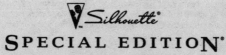

Silhouette®

SPECIAL EDITION

Published by Silhouette Books

America's Publisher of Contemporary Romance

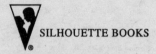

SILHOUETTE BOOKS

ISBN-13: 978-0-373-65445-1
ISBN-10:   0-373-65445-6

Recycling programs
for this product may
not exist in your area.

THE BRAVO BACHELOR

Copyright © 2009 by Christine Rimmer

All rights reserved. Except for use in any review, the reproduction
or utilization of this work in whole or in part in any form by any
electronic, mechanical or other means, now known or hereafter
invented, including xerography, photocopying and recording, or in
any information storage or retrieval system, is forbidden without
the written permission of the editorial office, Silhouette Books,
233 Broadway, New York, NY 10279 U.S.A.

This is a work of fiction. Names, characters, places and incidents are
either the product of the author's imagination or are used fictitiously, and
any resemblance to actual persons, living or dead, business establishments,
events or locales is entirely coincidental.

This edition published by arrangement with Harlequin Books S.A.

® and TM are trademarks of Harlequin Books S.A., used under license.
Trademarks indicated with ® are registered in the United States Patent
and Trademark Office, the Canadian Trade Marks Office and in other
countries.

Visit Silhouette Books at www.eHarlequin.com

Printed in U.S.A.

CHRISTINE RIMMER

came to her profession the long way around. Before settling down to write about the magic of romance, she'd been everything from an actress to a salesclerk to a waitress. Now that she's finally found work that suits her perfectly, she insists she never had a problem keeping a job—she was merely gaining "life experience" for her future as a novelist. Christine is grateful not only for the joy she finds in writing, but for what waits when the day's work is through: a man she loves, who loves her right back, and the privilege of watching their children grow and change day to day. She lives with her family in Oklahoma. Visit Christine at www.christinerimmer.com.

For Tom and Ed,
the sweetest guys I know—
well, on four legs, anyway.

Chapter One

That March morning, Mary Hofstetter dragged herself out of bed at dawn. It was going to be a beautiful, sunny day and Mary felt lousy. Her back ached. All night, the baby had played football with her rib cage. She'd gotten maybe two hours' sleep.

Mary trudged outside to feed the two aging horses, the chickens and the goats. Inside again, she prepared breakfast; she brewed herb tea, made toast and whipped up a protein shake.

The plan was to go straight to the computer once she'd eaten. Instead, she started cleaning. Nesting instinct, she told herself. After all, she was due in three weeks. She whipped the kitchen into shape, made her bed, dusted her bedroom and the living room. After that, she cleaned the shower and mopped the kitchen floor.

By then, it was a little after ten and the work that really

needed doing could no longer be put off. Strangely, in the past month or two, as her stomach had gotten bigger, her mind had gotten…dreamier. This was normal, she knew from her reading on pregnancy and childbirth, and would pass eventually after the baby came. Too bad that knowing she would someday have her focus back didn't help her meet her deadline now.

With a sigh of resignation, Mary sat down at the computer in the corner of the living room. Her two thousand-word article on canning summer fruit was due at *Ranch Life* magazine the next day. She'd have the article finished and e-mailed in by five if it killed her. Which, considering how tired and unfocused she was, it just might.

She booted up the PC—and stalled some more, fiddling with stuff on the desktop, straightening the tape dispenser and the stapler, moving the coffee mug full of pens from the left corner to the right. Another sigh and she made herself bring up the document she'd started yesterday.

Enjoy Summer's Bounty All Winter Long.

"Blah." Mary made a face at the title. And then she yawned. From the rug near the fireplace, her dog, Brownie, lifted her head and yawned, too. "I know, I know," she told the dog. "Bo-ring."

Then she scowled at the screen again. And shook her head. Later, if she finished with time to spare, she could stew over the title. Right now she needed to get some serious words on the page. She started typing.

Four sentences later, she heard the crunch of tires on gravel out in front. Brownie lifted her head again, gave a half-hearted "Woof," and then dropped her head back to her paws.

Mary wasn't expecting company, but hey, any excuse to get up from that desk sounded wonderful to her.

Groaning softly at the effort, she put her hands on the desktop and pushed herself to her feet. She arched her back to get the kinks out and then waddled over to the front window to see who'd dropped by.

Her visitor was still inside the car. It was a Cadillac SUV, that car. Black as a polished patent-leather shoe, with pricey gold rims that gleamed proudly in the Texas sun. It looked more than a little out of place in her dusty front yard.

Mary rubbed the base of her spine with one hand and supported her heavy belly with the other as she watched a tall man emerge from the fancy vehicle. Dark glasses covered his eyes. Though the vehicle blocked most of his body, she could see he wore a western shirt.

But the guy was no cowboy. If he were, he wouldn't be driving an Escalade with shining gold rims. And he certainly wouldn't be hauling out a briefcase and laying it on the roof of the car. Plus, something about the arrogant set of those broad shoulders spoke, loud and proud, of money and privilege. He stood for a moment without closing the door, his dark-gold head turned toward the house. Bright morning sun sparkled like stars on the lenses of his sunglasses.

Mary knew by then why he'd come. The Bravos must have sent him. Her tired shoulders slumped. So much for a nice diversion. She would rather be back at her desk, racking her fuzzy brain for a fascinating way to describe sterilizing canning jars, than dealing with the man who'd just taken off his sunglasses and tossed them casually to the seat of his pricey SUV.

He shut the driver's door, grabbed the briefcase and came around the front of the vehicle. Mary dug her fingers into the aching muscles at the base of her spine and wished he would just turn around, open that door again, get back in that beautiful car and drive off. How many times does a woman have to say "no" before the big-money types take the hint and go away?

As he mounted the steps to her front porch, she actually considered not answering his knock. After all, she was feeling like a beached whale, she'd already told the Bravos "no" three times and meant it—and she had work that truly did need doing.

But then, with a certain bittersweet sadness, she thought of Rowdy. Rowdy had always been the soul of politeness. Though he was fourteen years older than she was, he'd called her "ma'am" for weeks after they met—until their first date, as a matter of fact. A gentle, soft-spoken, old-fashioned man, he would always take off his hat in the presence of a woman.

Rowdy would never have given those Bravos what they were after. But he *would* do them the courtesy of answering the door and telling them "no" straight to their faces. Again.

So when the rich man knocked, Mary answered.

She pulled the door open and there he was, so handsome and fit-looking, he might have been a model. Or even a movie star. He had a sexy smile ready—a smile that only wavered slightly when he got a look at her ginormous stomach. Apparently, if someone back at the BravoCorp highrise in San Antonio had told him that the Hofstetter widow was pregnant, they'd failed to mention *how* pregnant.

He gestured for her to open the glass storm door that still stood between them. With a sigh, she flipped the lock and pushed it open a crack. He took the handle and pulled it the rest of the way until it caught and held wide.

"Mary Hofstetter?" He had a voice to match his looks. Deep and manly. Smooth as melted butterscotch.

She drew her shoulders back and forced a smile. "Yes?"

"I'm Gabe. Gabe Bravo." Well. Darned if they hadn't sent a real Bravo this time. He took out a card and handed it over.

Without giving it so much as a glance, she stuck the card in the back pocket of her jeans and got right down to the business of getting rid of him. "I'd invite you in, but I've got work that won't wait. And there's really no point in us talking, anyway. I'll only be telling you what I've told the others you sent. I don't care what the offer is, I'm not selling. So you have a nice day." She granted him a nod, parsed out a tight smile and started to shut the door.

"Mary." He spoke softly, but with clear command. His tone made her hesitate with the door half-closed. Sky-blue eyes reproached her—and somehow managed to gleam with wry humor at the same time. "You haven't even heard what I've come to say."

"I've heard enough from those other men you sent."

"But since then, we've rethought the offer. There's more now."

"Doesn't make a bit of difference."

He put on a hurt look. "How can you say that?"

Mary looked at him straight on. "Easily."

"You're making a big mistake. You don't know yet what we're willing to do to come to a satisfying solution to this problem."

"But, Gabe, I don't need to know. For me, there is no problem. I'm *already* satisfied."

"Come on." He wrapped his hand around the door frame, a supremely casual move. "Let me surprise you." His eyes were alight with humor, as if he *dared* her to shut the door now—and crush his tanned fingers with their buffed-smooth nails. "Please."

She stared into those gorgeous eyes and found herself thinking that maybe a surprise wouldn't be half-bad—and then she blinked and shook her head. "Seriously. I've already decided. I don't want to sell. Now, I really do have to—"

"You'll never be sure unless you hear me out." He slanted her a sideways look, mouth curved in a hint of a smile, as if they shared a secret, just the two of them.

She knew the guy was working her, knew she should simply say "no thank you," ask him to move his hand and shut the door the rest of the way. But she didn't. Nervously, she guided a few stray strands of hair away from her eyes, tucking them behind her ear. "No, really. I'm sorry you drove out here for nothing. But I just…don't have time right now."

He refused to give up. "I promise you," he coaxed. "It won't take long. Don't make me go back to my board of directors without being sure I've done all I can to change your mind." Another smile, a hopeful one.

Mary couldn't stop herself from smiling in return. What was it about him? She'd allowed the first guy they'd sent into the house. It had seemed only right to hear the offer before giving her answer. Once was enough, though. She hadn't let the other two past her front door.

But *this* guy…well, he did have a way about him. All smooth and sociable. Too good-looking to be real, much too slick—and yet somehow, he still managed to come across as down-to-earth. As if the two of them were longtime friends and he was just stopping by to see how she was getting along.

"I could make a pot of coffee, I guess…" The words came out almost of their own accord at the same time as she found herself stepping backward, opening the door wide.

"Mary." He granted her another of those I'm-your-best-friend smiles. "I think you must have read my mind."

Chapter Two

Gabe followed the Hofstetter widow through her living room, taking it all in—the worn, mismatched furniture, the scuffed hardwood floor, the scraggly-looking mutt sleeping in the corner, the cluttered desk and ancient PC. And the widow herself, in baggy jeans, red Keds and a white shirt shaped like a tent that billowed out over the giant bulge of her belly.

The floor plan was a simple one. An alcove near the front door held a narrow stairway and a half bath. The living room opened onto the single dining area, with a small U-shaped kitchen to the right of a square table. As he reached the table, he saw that a door opposite the kitchen led into a shadowed bedroom. He could see a rocking chair with a red bag hooked over the backrest, a pine night table and a section of a bed with a pine head-board.

"Have a seat." She gestured at the table as she turned to the kitchen nook.

Gabe took the straight-back chair she offered and watched her as she loaded up a coffee filter with grounds from a can and filled the reservoir with tap water. Her giant stomach pressed the tiled counter as she worked. And her brown hair needed a cut. She had it tied back in a sloppy ponytail from which limp strands escaped along her nape and around her face.

Once she had the coffeemaker going, she lumbered on over and took the chair opposite him, lowering herself into it with a soft grunt of effort. "All right," she told him once she was seated. "Coffee'll be ready in a minute."

"Thanks, Mary." He made his voice sincere and respectful, with just the right easy touch of warmth. Gabe was a master at reading people, at gauging how they saw themselves and how they wanted to be treated. It was part of his job as the family lawyer and so-called "fixer," the one they sent in when things weren't going as planned. Most women, whatever their age or marital status, liked a little harmless flirting from a man. They liked to be noticed and appreciated.

Not this woman. She preferred her interactions simple and direct and she didn't flirt with strangers. Gabe had known that at the door, the moment he gazed into those big brown eyes with the weary dark circles beneath them.

"You might as well go ahead and…" She stopped in mid-sentence. Wincing, she laid her hand on the side of her giant stomach.

Alarm had him sitting up straighter. "What is it, Mary?" Was she going to drop the kid right there at the table? "Is something wrong?"

She let out a long breath and patted the air between them with her palm. "No. It's fine. It's nothing. A cramp. Please. Can we get on with this?"

"Absolutely." He preferred to start out with at least a few minutes of conversation, to establish a better tone—less dry and rushed, more casual. And friendly. Most people found it hard to say no to a friend. But she wanted him to move it along. So he pretended to do that. He got out his laptop. "This'll just take a minute…" He aimed the back of the screen her way and punched a few keys, to make it look like he was setting things up.

She said, sounding really tired, "You know, you can stall all you want to, trying to figure out the most effective way to come at me, but it won't do you any good." She had leaned back in the chair and rested her hand on the swell of her stomach. Her eyes were closed and she spoke with the drowsy voice of someone seriously in need of a long nap. "I meant what I said to you at the door. *And* what I said to those three other guys you sent before. It makes no difference how much you offer me, I will never sell the Lazy H."

Never say never, Mary. "Why not?"

She opened her eyes and frowned at him. "It doesn't matter why not—except to me."

He studied her face for a moment, thinking that his job here would be easier if she were a little needier and not quite so smart. "Here's what matters," he told her. "Sell that overgrown hundred and twenty acres out there to Bravo-Corp at the price I'm going to offer you this morning and you'll be a wealthy woman. You—and your baby—will never want for anything for the rest of your lives. You can go to bed and get some rest when I leave because you won't have to work. Not today. Not ever again."

With another soft grunt, she sat a little straighter. "There
are worse things than not having a lot of money. And better
things than being rich. Things like a place you love to be.
Like having good people to care for, who care for you. This
ranch is the place I love to be. And as for having to work,
well, isn't that a lot of what life's about? It's true I'm pretty
beat today, but I like to work, most of the time. And if I
sold out to BravoCorp so you could carve the land my
husband loved into pricey half-acre lots, well, I'd never
forgive myself." The coffeemaker sputtered. She glanced
toward the sound.

"Let me." He half-rose.

"No." She waved him off and pushed herself upright.
"I'll do it. I don't mind at all." She went on over there and
got down a mug. "Milk and sugar?"

"Just black."

She filled the mug and brought it to him, her belly
leading the way. "There you go." Resting one hand on the
back of his chair, she set the mug beside his laptop. He
found himself staring at her throat, for some reason. Her
skin looked soft. A loose curl of hair curved against her
cheek. She smelled of soap and lemons—and she had seen
the laptop's screen. "Well, what do you know, Gabe? I
think it's finally all ready to go." She glanced at him, those
tired, dark eyes suddenly dancing.

Too damn smart, he thought. *Too smart by half.*

He pulled the nearest chair closer. "Sit down here." He
patted the seat. "Where you can see."

She sent him a look of ironic good humor. "It's not
going to matter if I can see that screen or not."

"Sit down, anyway. Listen to what I have to say, watch
what I have to show you."

With reluctance, she did. "All right, Gabe. Hit me with the pie charts and the tricolor graphs."

He sipped his coffee, made a sound of approval. "So many fancy ways to make coffee now. But I still prefer it fresh out of a can, brewed in a regular coffeemaker. Or boiled on an open fire, with eggshells at the bottom of the pot to cut the bitterness."

She folded her arms on top of her stomach. "Go out camping a lot, do you?"

"My family owns a ranch not far from here, Bravo Ridge. I've spent a lot of nights outside around a campfire, mostly when I was growing up."

"Brothers and sisters?"

"Six brothers, two sisters."

"Big family." She seemed surprised.

"That's right."

She asked, "You the oldest?"

"No, second born."

"So why don't you build your fancy houses on your own ranch?"

Had he seen that one coming? You bet he had. He sipped more coffee and told her why his family ranch wouldn't do—even if the family *had* been willing to let it go. "Bravo Ridge is too far from a major highway. The plan is to build a top-quality San Antonio bedroom community that's just far enough out to be considered in the country. With energy and oil prices so high, access and reasonable commute times are going to be key."

"Plus, it's your family ranch, right? Your…heritage. Your history. No way you'd let some developer build tract homes on it."

She had it right. He changed the subject. "Mary. Please.

Not tract homes. Each house will be one of a kind. It's a fine plan we've put together." He gestured toward the glass-topped back door. It opened onto a patio—he could see the rusting metal patio cover. Beyond that, across a rough patch of drying grass and a wide dirt driveway, there was a barn and a few other rundown outbuildings and pens. "Your land will be put to good use."

"My land is already put to good use."

He spoke gently again. "You're a freelance writer, Mary, not a rancher. We both know you barely have time to take care of the few animals your husband left you. With the baby coming, it's only going to get more difficult for you."

"I'll manage."

"Your land is overgrown."

"I like it that way."

It's dangerous *that way,* he thought. *A damn wildfire waiting to happen.* But she might take such a remark as some kind of veiled threat and that wasn't the tone he was going for. "I'm only saying that the land itself would be better served if it got more care."

Now she was studying him. "More care, huh?"

"That's right."

"You know, I can see why they send you in to make the impossible happen, to…how did they put it in the *Godfather* movies?"

He saluted her with the mug and reluctantly provided the words she was looking for. "Make them an offer they can't refuse?"

"That's it."

So much for avoiding any hint of a threat. "The Bravos are hardly the Mafia, Mary."

"Of course you're not." She rubbed the side of her big

stomach, frowning. "But you *are* used to getting what you want."

"And so are the people we deal with. We do our best to make every transaction a win-win."

She pulled a face at that. And then she shrugged. "Anyway, as I was saying…" Her brows drew together and she slid her hand around behind her to rub her lower back. "I can see why they sent you. There's something about you. It's partly your looks."

"Thanks. I think."

"I'm just stating a fact. It never hurts to be good-looking when you show up to try and charm a person into doing something she's repeatedly refused to do. And you *are* charming."

"I try."

"Well, it's working."

"Good to know."

"Plus, you seem…so calm. And patient. And interested, too. Interested in me and my welfare."

"I *am* interested, Mary." It was true. Not so much in her welfare. But in *her*. She wasn't what he'd expected. To bend her to his will, gently, so that in the end she decided she *wanted* to sell, would be a challenge. And challenges interested him. But the truth was, even if he *hadn't* been interested, he would have said he was and made her think he meant it.

She smoothed another lock of hair behind her ear. "I mean, we both know you're only trying to manipulate me into signing away my ranch."

"Ouch."

"But yet you seem so *relaxed* about it. As if you don't really care if you make it happen or not, as if you're just enjoying sitting here in my kitchen with me, drinking regular coffee that came out of a can."

"I *am* enjoying this, Mary." He leaned closer. Her scent drifted to him again: Ivory soap and citrus. He lowered his voice. "That's my secret. I enjoy making things…work out."

"Work out for BravoCorp, you mean."

"And for you, Mary. Believe it or not, I'm on your side."

She didn't roll her eyes, but she did make a small sound of disbelief.

He sat back in his chair. "Ready for the presentation?"

"As I'll ever be."

Mary couldn't hold back a laugh when the name of the housing development appeared on the screen.

Gabe punched the pause button. "What? You don't like the name?"

"Bravo River? There's no Bravo River on my property. There's no river at all."

"True. But there's a nice, wide creek."

"Skunk Creek, you mean?"

"That's the one. We'll change the name."

He wouldn't be doing any such thing, since he was not getting his hands on the Lazy H. But she'd already told him that about a hundred times, so she kept quiet. He punched the key again and the show continued.

In spite of herself, Mary was impressed. The presentation started with a great little movie. There was stirring music and a narrator who sounded like Robert Duvall.

The movie showed how BravoCorp, its architects and builders would respect the land when they built on it, designing each house to fit the terrain of the lot it would stand on, so that existing trees and geological features would remain, as much as possible, the way nature had created them. The houses themselves would employ green technology, using renewable resources, incorporating solar energy. There would even be Bravo River buses available between the development and San Antonio, so people could use mass transit rather than driving their cars and contributing to greenhouse gases and the oil crisis.

A montage of images showed the housing development taking shape, and then an aerial tour showed how it would look when it was completed. And even though she would never let it happen on her land, Mary had to admit, it was going to be beautiful when they finally found a place to put it.

He also had the pie charts and graphs she'd expected. They detailed how great Bravo River was going to be for the area, for the economy, for everybody—especially Mary. Now not only were they offering her a whopping price for the Lazy H, they were throwing in a percentage of the project's profits.

If there was any chance that Mary might have changed her mind, she would have done it after seeing Gabe's presentation. But there was no chance, as she'd made more than clear. She was only waiting for him to finish so she could say "no." Again.

Finally, the theme music swelled and the BravoCorp logo filled the screen.

Gabe gently reached out and pulled the laptop shut. "Let me answer your questions and then we'll—"

"No," Mary said. "Really. I don't have any questions."

"Well, all right." He bent to his briefcase and pulled out a sheaf of papers. "Let's go over the particulars."

Mary felt the strangest twinge in her back right then—

like a big rubber band snapping. Swallowing a gasp at the unpleasant sensation, she spread her legs to make room for her stomach and leaned forward, trying to stretch the weird feeling away. She rubbed the base of her spine some more. As she rubbed, she repeated what she'd told him way too many times already.

"Seriously, Gabe. It's not going to happen." She massaged the achy spot, but the ache only seemed to spread, slithering out from her spine on both sides. She bit back a groan as the twinges moved from beneath her ribs to the sides of her belly and kept going, encircling her giant waist like a belt, and then yanking tight. Somehow, she managed to speak in an even, clear tone in spite of the pain. "I've made it more than clear that I'll never sell."

Gabe behaved as if he hadn't heard her. He set the stack of papers on the table and rapped his knuckles on them. "I think we should go through these. What can it hurt?"

"But there's no point." Trying hard to ignore the pains and keep her voice firm and reasonable, she explained, "I will raise my child here. I love it here. I'm not leaving—and besides, my husband loved this place, too. I swear Rowdy would turn over in his grave if I ever gave up his beloved Lazy H to be carved into little plots, each with its own spacious and gracious McMansion on it."

Gabe Bravo didn't miss a beat. "You're not getting it, Mary. We're not talking about any cookie-cutter McMansions. Each home at Bravo River will be one-of-a-kind. And constructed with care and concern for the land and the environment." His blue eyes changed, grew soft with sincerity. "And I am so sorry that you've lost your husband." He really did sound like he meant it. He coaxed, "Mary. Come on. I can't believe your husband would want you to pass up an offer like this, especially considering that you're about to have a child. I know if Rowdy were here, he would be thinking that his baby should have all the good things money can buy. His baby—*your* baby—deserves a broadened horizon. That means the choice of elementary and high schools. And college. When the time comes, you'll be able to foot the bill for the very best in higher education without having to think twice. Mary, if Rowdy were here, I know he would surprise you with what he would do for you and your baby, with the choice that he would make, the choice for your future, for the kind of security you'll have with a fortune in the bank."

Mary masked her increasing discomfort and put on her sweetest smile. "Since you never knew my husband, how can you possibly know what he might have wanted? And the truth is, I love this place as much as Rowdy ever did. Maybe more. I'm doing all right and my baby will be just fine, thank you. And now, well, I've enjoyed visiting with you, Gabe, but seriously. I have to get back to work."

He looked at her steadily. "Are you kicking me out, Mary?"

"That's right, Gabe. I am."

He slipped the papers in the briefcase. His laptop followed. He slanted her a look as he snapped the latches shut. "You know I'll be back, right?"

"And after this, I won't be offering any coffee. You won't get past the door again, so don't waste your time. Please."

"Don't worry, Mary. I never waste my time." Briefcase in hand, he rose.

Mary pushed herself upright, too, with effort. The weird cramping was worse than before. And all at once, she was sweating, at her hairline, on her upper lip and under her arms.

And the cramps really were bad. They scared her, shooting around her distended belly from the now-constant pain in her back. It hurt so much, she had to grab the back of the chair to keep from crumpling to the floor. A soft cry escaped her.

"Mary." Gabe's voice came to her. He sounded really worried. Gabe Bravo. Mr. Smooth. Worried. Somehow, that scared her more than anything. More than the sudden sweat dripping down her face. More than the horrible, squeezing pain. "Mary, what's wrong?"

She couldn't talk, couldn't answer. She clutched the chair back, groaning.

And then something shifted down low inside her. A dropping sensation, as if someone had bounced a boulder on the floor of her womb. She let out a guttural cry as she felt the wetness in her panties. It couldn't be....

But it was.

Her water had broken.

Chapter Three

Handsome, clever Gabe Bravo was looking at her strangely.

He said her name again, with urgency. "Mary!" His briefcase hit the floor with a smack as he lunged to catch her before she fell. She collapsed against him, moaning.

So embarrassing. To be groaning like this, holding her belly, sweating profusely—and leaning on this rich, slick stranger. But she couldn't help it. If she didn't let him hold her up, she would be on the floor.

Sagging in his strong arms, she felt the wetness as it dripped out of her. Not a flood. Uh-uh. More of an ooze. A slimy dribble. Mary shuddered at the icky feel of it.

"You're shaking," Gabe said. "What the hell is going on?"

She looked up to meet his worried eyes. "My, um, my water just broke. I think I have to go and have my baby…."

His bronze brows drew together. "Now?"

"Yes. I think so. Now."

"You're serious."

"I certainly am." Another cramp took her, this one worse than the last. Stronger. More overwhelming. "Aungh..." All she could do was clutch her belly with one hand and his arm with the other and groan like something not quite human.

He didn't leave her. He stayed there, holding her up as the cramp crested and finally began to recede. When the pain eased, as she panted and sweated in the aftermath of it, he said, "Come on. Let's get you comfortable."

"Comfortable?" She looked at him with horror. She didn't even know him, and he was going to make her comfortable? *Rowdy,* she cried inside. *Oh, Rowdy. I need you. I need you so bad. Why aren't you here?* What she said was, "I...no. I'll be fine. Really. And you need to go."

"Come on," he said again, as if she hadn't spoken. He started for the living room, guiding her along, his arm around her waist, keeping her upright at the same time as he urged her forward.

"Did you hear what I said?" She tried to jerk away.

He held on. "I heard you. And I'm not leaving. Not until you've called for help."

Okay. He had a point. She was in no condition to be left alone. And as she shuffled away from the table, she realized she didn't dare let go of him, after all. Another cramp might come. She would end up on the floor.

The short walk, as she clung to him, stumbling along, panting, still leaking fluid under her jeans, seemed to take forever. When they got there, he helped her to sit, holding on to steady her as she lowered herself.

Halfway down to the sofa cushions, she let out a yelp. "No! I don't think I can...really, I can't..." What was she saying?

She had no idea. "Oh, I'm so scared. This isn't supposed to be…not now. Too early. I have three weeks yet…"

"Shh," he said, so softly. "Mary. It's all right. Whatever's going on, you'll get through it. You will. You're going to be fine…"

"Fine?" She stared at him, frantic, sweat in her eyes. "Fine?" She spat the word at him.

"Yes. Fine." His blue gaze didn't waver. "Now, come on. Sit down. You can do it. Come on…"

And somehow, she did do it. Clutching his arm like a lifeline, she allowed him to guide her the rest of the way down.

"Good," he said softly, when at last she was seated. "Now, let's take off your shoes and you can stretch out."

"No!" She slapped his gentle hand away and pressed her legs together in an attempt to hide the dark stains on her jeans. While she was staggering here from the kitchen, the fluid had run all the way down into her Keds. She was not taking off her shoes, all wet and sticky, in front of a man she'd met less than an hour ago.

Mary groaned low again. The groan deepened to an animal growl as the next cramp struck. She grabbed his hand tight again, suddenly needing the contact. So what if she didn't know him? He was there and that was everything. Curling over herself, one hand under her belly, the other holding tight to Gabe Bravo, she moaned long and loudly.

Somewhere in the middle of that one, he said, "I'll call an ambulance."

"No." She clutched his hand for dear life, squeezing it till she heard the finger joints pop. "Wait. Stay. You have to…one minute…"

When the cramping passed that time, she panted out instructions. "Phone. Over there. On the desk." He got it and gave it to her. "Doctor," she said, wheezing like a winded horse. "Calling my doctor...."

"All right. Great idea." He stood there beside her, waiting, as she autodialed the number.

Dr. Breitmann came right to the phone. She told him about her water breaking and he asked how far apart her contractions were. When she said she could hardly tell as there hadn't been that many, he chuckled.

"You're going to be fine, Mary," the doctor said. "Just head on over to the hospital. I'll meet you there and we'll see what's going on."

"I'm..." She turned away from the stranger looming over her and spoke low into the phone. "I'm all wet."

"You can go ahead and change." Dr. Breitmann said. "And clean up a little, if you wish. Not a bath. But you can wipe off with a damp cloth and then use a sanitary napkin. Amniotic fluid will probably continue to escape."

"Ugh," she said in response to that bit of news.

"You'll be okay," he reassured her again. "We don't want to fool around with this, but it isn't what you'd call an emergency."

Surely she hadn't heard right. "It isn't?"

"Mary, in spite of what you see in the movies, it can sometimes be days before delivery after the water breaks."

"You're kidding."

"I'm not. So take a deep breath and calm down."

"All right. Yes. I will."

"Just get yourself ready and come on to the hospital."

When she hung up, Gabe was still looming above her. He demanded, "What did he say?"

She told him—though really, it was none of his business. "I…have to clean up a little. And then I have to go to the hospital. I'm going to be fine. Thank you for…being so great about this."

"Not a problem."

She waited, figuring he would get the message and get out. But he only looked at her, not budging, leaving her no choice but to tell him outright, "So, then. You should go."

"Not until the ambulance gets here. Give me the phone and I'll—"

"Uh-uh." She pressed it to her chest. "You should go."

From a pocket, he produced one of those devices that does everything but your laundry. "As soon as the ambulance gets here."

She grabbed his hand before he could dial 911. "No ambulance. I don't need one."

The look in his eyes said he thought she was out of her mind. But he did put the device away. "Are you saying you have someone to drive you?"

She groaned and hunched over her stomach as the next contraction began. He waited, standing close beside her, as it crested and finally eased off. Once she could think again, she raised her gaze to his. "No ambulance," she repeated, in case he hadn't gotten the message the first two times she said it. An ambulance would cost more than she was ready to pay. She had insurance to cover the hospital and the birth, but not an optional ride with the EMTs. "Dr. Breitmann said this wasn't an emergency, so an ambulance isn't necessary."

"Looks pretty damn necessary to me." His square jaw was set.

"You're not the decider on this. You need to—"

"Forget it." He glared down at her. "I'm going nowhere. Not until your ride gets here." He gestured at the phone she still clutched in her hand. "Go ahead. Call them. Tell them to get over here, fast."

Mary shut her eyes and sucked in a slow breath through her nose.

He pressed her, as determined about this as he'd been about his pricey housing development. "You *do* have someone to drive you, don't you?"

She drew herself up. "Of course, I have someone who's supposed to drive me. My mother-in-law, Ida."

"Good. Then call her. I'll wait with you until she arrives. How far away is she?"

Mary gulped. "Well…"

"Where is your ride?" He said each word slowly, as if he doubted her ability to comprehend the question.

And she was forced to confess, "Ida's in St. Louis. Her sister's been sick. And please don't look at me like that. I do have a ride. It's all arranged. It's just…I'm not due for three weeks. Ida was going to be home before the baby came."

He sat down next to her on the sofa and touched the side of her face, guiding a sweaty tendril of hair out of her eye. Funny, but it didn't bother her at all that he did that. She found his touch comforting, somehow. It steadied her.

"Mary." He said her name so gently.

She tossed the phone to the sofa cushions and let out a moan. "Oh, this can't be happening. Not today. Ida's gone. And I have a deadline…"

"Mary."

She made herself meet his eyes. "What?"

"Do what you need to do. Get your stuff."

"And clean up. Really, I *have* to clean up."

"Fine. Do it. And then I'll drive you to the hospital."

She gasped. "Oh, no. It's too much. You don't have to. Really."

"You won't take an ambulance and your ride's in St. Louis. Do not try and tell me that you'll be driving yourself."

"I'm not. There are, um, neighbors I could call. And there's—"

"Mary. Stop."

"Oh, dear Lord…" She just couldn't think.

But *he* could. He knew what to do. "Go. Get ready. And we'll be on our way."

Satisfied that he'd finally convinced Mary to let him take her where she needed to go, Gabe waited beside her through another of those grueling contractions.

"Help me to my bedroom?" she asked him when it was over.

"You got it. Where is it?" He helped her up again.

She pointed toward the dining area. "In there. Opposite the kitchen…"

He walked her back there to the door on the left that led into her room. She got a change of clothes and disappeared into the bathroom.

She seemed to take a long time in there. That worried him. When over five minutes had passed, he knocked on the door. "You all right?"

"Yeah. Fine. Don't you dare come in."

"You need to get going. Don't fool around in there."

"Gabe?"

"Yeah?"

"I hate you." She muttered the words, probably thinking he couldn't hear them. Then, louder, "Never mind."

He smiled to himself. "Just move it along."

Maybe two minutes later, she emerged wearing clean clothes and carrying a stack of fresh towels. "I thought we might need these—you know, in your fancy car."

God, he hoped not. "Good thinking." He took them from her.

"And I have a suitcase all ready," she said.

"Where?"

"Under the bed."

So he set the towels on the bedspread and got down on his knees to drag it out for her. "I'll just take this stuff to the car," he said, rising. He picked up the stack of towels and hoisted the old hard-sided suitcase in his free hand.

She hobbled over and got the big, red shoulder bag from where it was hooked on the back of an old rocking chair. "Diaper bag." She slid it onto his shoulder.

"Back in a flash," he promised.

She pressed her lips together and nodded, reaching out to grasp the back of the rocker as another cramp started.

"Mary…" He took a step toward her.

She made a frantic waving-off motion with her free hand. "Go. Hurry. I'll be…" She groaned. Hard. "Fine…"

He made himself leave her, turning and racing through the house, pausing only long enough to set down the suitcase and throw open the front door.

Outside, the Escalade waited, gleaming in the sun. The sight of it stunned him. He'd climbed out of it such a short time ago, certain of his ability to bend the Hofstetter widow to his will and the will of BravoCorp.

Somehow, things had gotten away from him—gotten away, big-time. In his pocket, his BlackBerry started vibrating. He went to the back and lifted the hatch and tossed in the suitcase and the diaper bag.

Then he took out the phone and glanced at the display. It was his father. Eager for a report on his meeting with the widow, no doubt.

You don't want to know, Dad. He let the call go to voice mail and was putting the device away when it started vibrating again. This time he didn't even stop to glance at it, just tucked it in his pocket and carried the towels to the backseat on the far side, where he left them, neatly stacked. In case she ended up needing them—a thought that made his gut clench.

He sent a fervent glance heavenward. He wasn't a guy who prayed much, but he prayed then. *Just let us make it to the hospital before she has that baby. Just that. It's all I ask....*

He ran around the front of the car, across the dusty yard and up the front steps. Inside again, he found her waiting in the open archway to the kitchen, slumped against the wall there. She was panting, staring at the floor. But when she heard him enter, she looked up, wiped her sweating brow and forced a smile.

"Got my purse..." She touched the strap over her shoulder and smiled wider, a smile that wobbled only a little.

"Good." He strode toward her. "Let's get the hell out of here."

"Wait."

He stopped in mid-step. "What now?"

"Brownie." The dog sat by the sofa. At the mention of her name, she stretched and wagged her tail. "She has a doggy door, in the laundry room off the kitchen. But if you could check her water bowl and pour her some food." She gestured weakly over her shoulder. "Food's in the cabinet next to the sink...."

He detoured around her and did what she asked. The dog

came right over to sniff the bowl and eat a few lumps of dry food. He petted her on the head and then put the bag of food back in the cabinet.

"Okay," he said, shutting the low door and rising. "Time to go."

He went to her and wrapped an arm around her, noting abstractly that the lemon and soap scent of her had changed. Now, she smelled like…cleanser, of all things, a sweet sort of smell.

They hobbled to the door and out. She stopped to lock it, and the storm door as well, then leaned on him as they went down the steps and out to the car. He had the door open and her up in the backseat before he remembered he'd left his briefcase where he'd dropped it, halfway under the table, on the kitchen floor.

Too bad. He'd have to come back for it later. Right now, the goal was to get Mary to the hospital. ASAP.

He got in without noticing he'd left his Ray-Bans on the seat. They snapped as he sat on them. He swore and pulled them out from under him. Both lenses had popped out. He tossed the pieces onto the empty seat beside him and started up the engine.

In the back, Mary groaned and panted. He waited until she seemed to quiet—which meant she was between contractions—before he asked, "Where are we going?"

A breathless sound escaped her. "You…know Wulf City?"

It was blessedly close, maybe ten miles from there, just south of New Braunfels off I-35. "I know it. The name of the hospital?"

"Wulf City Memorial." She rattled off an address.

He punched the information into the dashboard GPS. A moment later, the electronic map showed him where to go and the canned voice began giving instructions. He drove the SUV in the circle of driveway that went around her house. Her dog was sitting on the back patio, looking kind of lost.

He heard Mary whisper, "See you later, girl," as they left the mutt behind.

In the backseat, Mary was hardly aware that they were merging onto the highway. She had one hand, white-knuckled, on the armrest. The other was down low, holding her belly, her legs spread wide, all modesty forgotten.

She had a faraway awareness that Mr. Smooth, Gabe Bravo, had practically carried her, leaking, moaning and panting, to his fancy car. She probably should have been mortified.

But by then, she was pretty much beyond mortification. Actually, between the excruciating, never-ending contractions, when she could think again, she was grateful. That he was there. That she hadn't ended up doing this impossible job alone.

Her heart hurt, knowing that Rowdy wasn't behind that wheel instead. That he'd died before he even knew they were finally going to have the baby they'd been trying for since they got married. When she closed her eyes, she could still see his beloved, craggy face and hear his rough voice.

Oh, she did miss the way he would call her "sweetheart," so shyly, with that look of adoration and wonder in his kind hazel eyes. She could see him as he left her that last time, kissing her at the sink and then going out the back door to check some fences, favoring his right leg, which had been injured in some long ago rodeo accident.

"Rowdy, oh, Rowdy…" She was crying, the tears streaming down her cheeks. She tasted them, salty, on her tongue. And she must have said Rowdy's name out loud, because Gabe turned around in the front seat.

"Mary. It's okay. Almost there..."

She dashed the tears away and tried to sit up straight. "No problem. Really. I'm doing fine back here." Another contraction struck. Gabe turned back to the road and Mary concentrated on riding out the pain.

After the time he turned around and saw the tears running down Mary's face as she cried for her lost husband, Gabe kept his eyes on the road. He figured if there was an emergency going on in the backseat, she would let him know.

Otherwise, better to give the poor woman a little privacy. It had to be hard to have a baby without your husband. He guessed. It wasn't the kind of thing he knew much about. Not being a woman, in the first place—and being a total bachelor, in the second. Gabe just didn't see the point of marriage and settling down with one woman. Well, for other guys, sure. But not for him. He liked women and they liked him. And he was real fond of variety. He never hung around one woman all that long. He enjoyed his freedom and he liked to keep his options open.

Behind him, Mary moaned in agony. And Gabe stopped thinking about how much he enjoyed being single and concentrated on getting to the hospital fast.

The ride seemed interminable, but it really wasn't that long. Nine minutes after leaving Mary's place behind, he was pulling into the turnaround in front of Wulf City Memorial, under a wide porte cochere. They had a wheelchair waiting in the vestibule behind the first set of glass doors. An orderly wheeled it out, another orderly at his side.

Gabe helped Mary out of the car and the orderlies settled her into the chair.

"Thank you," she told him, hooking her purse over her shoulder. "Thank you so much…" And one of the orderlies turned the chair around and wheeled her through the doors. The other followed, with the suitcase and the red diaper bag.

Gabe knew it was time to leave her. He'd done what he could for her. No one was going to fault him if he got back behind the wheel and got the hell out of there.

He could stop by her house in a couple of days. Mentally, he catalogued the contents of the briefcase he'd left under her table: nothing in there he couldn't do without for forty-eight hours. Everything on the laptop was on his computer at the office and most of it was on his Black-Berry, too. It would be perfect. He could visit after she got home from the hospital, see how she was doing, give her the towels that were still in the backseat, pick up the briefcase, admire her new baby. And continue with his campaign to get her to sell the Lazy H.

His BlackBerry vibrated again. He got it out and checked to see who it was: Carly Madison, his date of last Saturday night. They'd attended a dinner, a high-profile event to raise money for cancer research. Black tie. And then they'd gone to his place for a private party of their own….

And he couldn't stop worrying about Mary.

He glanced up at the doors they'd wheeled her through. Somehow, it just didn't seem right to him, to leave her alone in the hospital, without a friend or a relative to look after her.

He put the BlackBerry away unanswered and went to park his car. Five minutes later, he was pushing his way through the two sets of glass doors.

Chapter Four

Mary was still in reception, still sitting in that wheelchair. They'd wheeled her into the waiting area and left her there, her suitcase and diaper bag at her feet. Someone had given her a clipboard and a pen and she was trying to fill out a damn form, of all things.

He went to her. "What is going on?"

She let out a cry of surprise and almost dropped the clipboard. "Gabe. Wh...what are you doing here?"

"I decided it was a bad idea to drive off and leave you alone."

"But I'm not alone." She gestured with the pen, indicating the others in the reception area with her, and the counter with the clerks behind it. "There's a whole hospital full of people here to take care of me and you don't need to—"

"What is this?" He took the clipboard from her and riffled the forms clipped to it. "There must be ten pages of crap here."

"Give that back." She grabbed for it.

He held it out of her reach. "It's no time to be filling out forms. You need to be in a hospital bed. You're having a baby. Don't any of these people realize that?" He started for the front desk.

She called him back. "Gabe."

He hesitated, and made a low, disapproving sound to let her know he was listening.

"It's just procedure. Since this is happening earlier than planned, I'm not pre-admitted. So I have to fill out the forms. *Then* they admit me. And the longer you kick up dust about it, the longer until I get the paperwork out of the way and they take me to an examining room."

He dropped into the chair next to her. "This isn't right."

"Gabe." She glared at him. "Give me the…" The sentence became a groan as another contraction struck.

"Damn it, Mary." He offered his hand. She took it and set about grinding the bones.

When that one passed off, she whispered between clenched teeth, "Give me the clipboard. Now."

He saw that a compromise was in order. "How about this? I'll read you the questions and write them down for you…."

She made a growling sound. But she did give in. "Fine. Whatever. Do it."

"All right." He read down the page to where she'd stopped and then asked the next question. "Ever smoke cigarettes?"

"No."

"Drink alcohol?"

"Not in the past eight months."

"We'll call that a no…"

They were finished in about three minutes. He wheeled Mary up to the desk and the clerk took the clipboard.

The woman thumbed through the forms, nodded, and sent them a disinterested glance. "Have a seat. We'll call you in a few minutes."

Gabe opened his mouth to tell the clerk that "a few minutes" was completely unacceptable. He wanted Mary in the business end of that hospital and he wanted her there now.

But Mary tugged on his hand. "Gabe. No." He glanced down into her upturned face. The look in her eyes made it more than clear that he was not allowed to ream the clerk a new one. "I'm fine," she said firmly. "Okay? Fine."

So he wheeled her back to the waiting area, figuring if they didn't come get her good and soon, he'd be kicking some ass and taking some serious names—whether Mary wanted him to or not.

They did come a few minutes later, just as the clerk had promised, two women in scrubs. "Mrs. Hofstetter?" At Mary's nod, the shorter of the two women took charge of the chair. "Let's go, then."

They wheeled her through the double steel doors and he went with them, carrying her suitcase, her purse and the diaper bag. No one seemed to question his right to be with her.

The taller of the two women took his arm as the other wheeled Mary on down the corridor. "Mr. Hofstetter?"

Since explaining the situation might get him kicked out, he simply answered, "Yeah?"

"We'll take a brief history of your wife's labor so far and Dr. Breitmann will examine her. After that, if he determines she *is* having the baby today, she'll be moved to a labor room and you can stay with her there."

He didn't get the "if" part. It seemed pretty obvious to him that today was the day. But he didn't ask questions.

His job had been to get them to take care of her. Now that was accomplished, he was going with the theory that they knew what they were doing.

The nurse said, "Hold on to her things for now, why don't you?" She indicated a row of chairs against the hallway wall to their left. "You can make yourself comfortable there until we come for you."

"Uh. Right. Good enough…"

"Now's the time to make a few calls if you need to. Let the family know what's going on."

For a moment, he flashed on his father's face. Davis Bravo would be pretty damn surprised to know what was going on.

But of course, she didn't mean *his* family. She meant Mary's—about which he knew virtually nothing.

He faked it. "Good idea. I'll make a few calls."

So he sat in one of the chairs, with Mary's stuff around him, and got out his BlackBerry, for lack of anything better to do. He checked messages. There were several, including one from his Dad and one from Carly.

He listened to the first one, left by his father.

"Gabe. I'm getting impatient here. Call me when you get this. I want details on how it went. I want you to tell me the widow has sold us that ranch. There'll be no opportunity at lunch to—"

He clicked out of voice mail. He just didn't want to hear it. And calling his dad back was out of the question. Davis would start right in with his twenty questions routine: *How did it go? Is she on? Why not? Where are you now? You're* what?

Uh-uh. No, thanks. Not now. His father could wait. And he'd get back to Carly later, too. And the others. Right now, it all had to be about Mary, who was probably having a baby today, with no one from her family to be with her.

Ida, he thought. That was the mother-in-law's name. Maybe he should try and get in touch with Ida Hofstetter and tell her what was going on.

If he only had a clue what Ida's sister's name was, he could call St. Louis information….

He opened Mary's purse and felt around in there, feeling pretty creeped out about going through her personal stuff. But he did find a flip cell phone.

He checked her contacts. She had three numbers for her mother-in-law: Home, Store, Cell. He tried the cell and got sent to voice mail and left a message, giving his name and saying he'd driven Mary to the hospital, that Mary was fine, but that her mother-in-law should call Mary's cell or his cell or the hospital as soon as possible. He rattled off his cell number then hung up.

Then he tried Ida Hofstetter's home number, where he left a similar message. After that, he went ahead and tried the number called "Store."

A woman answered. "Hofstetter's Hardware. Donna Lynn speakin'."

From Donna Lynn, who it turned out was a clerk at Ida's store right there in Wulf Creek, he got Ida's sister's number in St. Louis and Donna Lynn's promise that she would have Ida call the hospital if she heard from her.

"You give Mary a big congratulations from me, you hear?"

"Well, she hasn't had the baby yet…."

"But when she does."

"I will, Donna Lynn. I promise."

"And I'll come by, tomorrow—I mean, if the hospital says the baby's arrived."

"Great."

"Uh. Who are you, now?"

A nurse was coming toward him. "Long story. Thanks, Donna Lynn." He disconnected the call with a sigh of relief.

The nurse led him to a room with a hospital bed and a couple of easy chairs. There was a door to a bathroom and curtains on the windows. Mary lay in the bed, wearing a flower-print hospital gown.

She looked happy to see him. "Gabe."

"How you doing?"

She blew out a slow breath. "Well, it's official. Dr. Breitmann says today's the day."

He set her things on the floor by the door and went to her. "Everything's okay, then?"

She nodded. "He says I'm in labor and everything is going well."

"But you told me it was too early…."

"It's okay. It's earlier than expected, but Dr. Breitmann says it's going to be all right, that the baby is capable of survival outside the womb."

"Good."

She waited until the nurse left to whisper, "They think you're my husband. They seem to have no clue that I'm on my own."

"Why would they? I didn't see a space for 'widow' in all those reams of paperwork." He took her hand and twined their fingers together. It seemed a totally appropriate thing to do at that moment. "And besides, you're not on your own. I'm here. It's not ideal, I know. But it's better than nothing."

"Gabe." She tried to look stern. "Seriously. There is no reason that you have to—"

"Yeah, there is. You need a friend right now."

A low laugh escaped her. "We're not friends."

"Sure we are."

She squeezed his hand. "You're really impressing me, you know that?"

"I do what I have to do."

"You're being amazing. But I have to say this right up front. No matter how wonderful you are today, you'll never get me to sell my ranch."

"Tell you what." He still had her cell, so he opened her fingers and wrapped them around it.

She frowned down at it. "What?"

"Let's forget about Bravo River. At least until your baby's born."

A shy smile curved her lips. "Deal—and what were you doing with my phone?"

"Stealing the numbers out of it. I called your mother-in-law at home and on her cell. Left messages. I also called her store, where the clerk answered. Donna Lynn wishes you well. She gave me Ida's sister's number. I saved it into your phone. So you can try to reach your mother-in-law there."

"I will…in a minute. Take this." She shoved the phone at him, threw back the sheet and swung her bare legs over the edge of the bed.

"Mary. What the…?"

But then she groaned and curved over her belly. And he understood. It was another contraction.

He gave her his hand again to hold onto, and she got through it as she had the ones before, supporting her big stomach with the hand that wasn't clutching his, groaning as if she was about to push that baby out right then and there.

When she could talk again, she swung her feet back on

the bed, covered up and took the cell back. She dialed and shook her head at him as the phone on the other end rang and rang. In the end, she left a message and flipped the phone shut. "Well. One way or another, Ida's bound to get the message that her grandchild is on the way." She set the phone on the stand by the bed.

In his pocket, his BlackBerry started vibrating.

She could hear the buzzing sound it made and slanted him a sideways look. "Aren't you going to answer that?"

About then, he realized it just might be Mary's mother-in-law. But when he got it out and checked the display, he saw it was only his father. Again. "It's nothing that can't wait." He put the phone away and pulled one of the easy chairs close. "What happens next?"

She reached for his hand. "More of the same. Hours of it."

He sat in the chair. "Having a baby is pretty damn monotonous."

She grinned at him, still holding tight to him, her fingers laced with his. "You're right. Well, aside from the screaming and the blood and the pain."

The hours went by. Nurses came and went. The doctor appeared twice, to ask Mary questions and examine her to see how her labor was progressing. Gabe wasn't really up on things like dilation and effacement, but he gathered that it was all happening pretty much as expected.

It seemed completely natural to him, to be there, holding Mary's hand, while Dr. Breitmann examined her. Natural, and important, too.

The whole process filled him with awe. And being awed wasn't like him. Not like him in the least. He found himself thinking stuff he never really thought about.

How he'd always been the kind of guy who skimmed along the surface of life, keeping it cool, never getting too close. He was self-aware enough to know that some people called him shallow, and self-assured enough not to give a damn what anyone thought. He liked his life just the way it was and he had no intention of changing it.

But there in that labor room, with Mary…

He was involved. *Really* involved. And it was great. Because this *mattered,* a new life coming. He wanted to help. Any damn way he could.

When they finally decided it was time to wheel Mary down to the delivery room, a nurse told him he'd have to suit up before he could go.

No problem, he said. Whatever they needed him to do. First, though, they had him take Mary's stuff into the room where she'd be staying after the birth. Once he did that, he put on the blue gown they gave him and the ridiculous hairnet, too, and he washed his hands with their special disinfecting soap.

And then they let him in to be with her. He got the top half of her, while the nurses and the doctor worked below. He held her hand when she needed it and wiped her sweaty face with a cool, wet cloth and said soothing things. He took his cue from the doctor and encouraged her when it was time to push.

And then, finally, after hours and hours of waiting, of Mary working like a trouper to make it happen, she pushed for all she was worth and Dr. Breitmann said, "This is it, I see the head…"

And Mary was panting and pushing and crying and Gabe heard himself say, "You're doing it, Mary. Come on. It's really happening…"

And she let out a low, agonized scream. Tears were running down her red, sweat-shiny, scrunched-up face as she pushed. And she let out a laugh, right then, at the same time as she was bawling her eyes out. "Lord. Gabe. I can't…"

"You can," he told her. "You are. You're doing great…."

She cried and laughed and pushed even harder and the nurse said the head was out. Mary pushed some more.

And then the doctor announced, "We've got the shoulders clear. The rest should be quick."

And it was. The baby slid out in a rush after that.

Gabe heard a raspy intake of breath and the baby's first cry, a loud, very cranky sound.

Mary said, "The baby? My baby…"

"You have a beautiful baby girl," said the doctor.

Mary cried, "Oh! Oh, thank you. Thank you…" as if Dr. Breitmann had done all that pushing and panting. She held out her arms.

The doctor passed her the baby. Mary cradled the tiny, squalling, blood-streaked, naked child close, not even caring that the cord was still attached.

She looked up at Gabe over the baby's head, through exhausted eyes that still managed to shine with pure happiness. "I can't believe it. I did it. Oh, Gabe. Look what I did…"

"You did good," he answered gruffly, around the sudden tightness in his throat. "Real good."

She stroked the baby's slimy, bloody head. "Virginia Mae," she whispered, and glanced at him again. "My mom was Virginia. And Ida's middle name is Mae."

"I like it," Gabe told her. "It's a fine name."

A few minutes later, the nurses clamped the cord and took the baby to examine her and clean her up a little.

Once they had her wrapped in a blanket, Gabe was allowed to hold her, just for a minute.

She was so light in his arms, and warm. He looked down into her squinty blue eyes and something…happened inside him, something momentous and scary, a feeling he didn't understand.

But so what? Why wouldn't he be gone on that baby? He'd just seen her being born. Even helped, as much as he could.

"Little Ginny," he whispered to her, and she made a happy cooing sound, as if she thought his nickname for her was just fine. He watched, fascinated, as she tried to get her fist into her little pink mouth.

By then, they were ready to take Mary and the baby to their room. They put Mary on a gurney and wheeled her down there while one of the nurses pushed the baby in a plastic hospital bassinet. Gabe trailed along behind, thinking vaguely that he probably should be getting going—but somehow, still not ready to leave Mary and the baby on their own.

Her room had two beds, but the other bed was empty, the privacy curtain pulled back. Once they had her settled, they raised the head of Mary's bed and she nursed Ginny for the first time, easing aside her hospital gown and putting the tiny red baby to her full white breast. The baby rooted around, making funny squeaky sounds. And then Mary guided the nearly-bald head into position, lifting her breast and offering the nipple at the same time. Ginny latched on and Mary said, "Ouch! That hurts…" And then she laughed softly to herself. "Well, I think you're catching on, aren't you?" She stroked Ginny's wispy hair.

Should Gabe have looked away while she fed her baby for the first time?

Yeah. Probably.

But he didn't. By then, he'd seen most of what there was to see of Mary Hofstetter. And it just wasn't…like that, with Mary. She was so natural about everything, so matter-of-fact. She had no false modesty.

She looked up from the baby at her breast and saw him watching her. And she smiled.

He smiled back and then her attention was all for Ginny again. Gabe watched that. The miracle of that. Mary and her baby, together.

Somewhere, a cell started ringing.

Mary looked up. "That's mine."

He got her purse out of the locker across the room and found the phone, which by then had gone silent.

"I'll bet it was Ida," Mary said.

He checked the display. "Sure enough."

"Hand it here. I'll call her back."

He gave her the phone. "I'll just get some coffee…"

She nodded, pressing the key to return the call, putting the phone to her ear with one hand, holding Ginny with the other, looking tired but happy as he slipped out.

He was just out the door when a ward clerk approached with a tray of food. "Is she awake?" the woman asked.

Gabe nodded and held the door for her.

Giving Mary a little time to talk to her baby's grandma in private, Gabe got coffee and a sandwich in the cafeteria. He wolfed down the food, suddenly realizing that he was starving. His BlackBerry buzzed while he was sitting there. He ignored it, though the soft sound seemed to nag at him. It reminded him that he was getting a little bit overboard about this, that it was way past time he told Mary he was leaving and got back to his own damn life.

He glanced at his Rolex. Seven-fifteen. He rubbed his grainy eyes and wondered at how the day had raced by with him hardly aware it was passing. He'd missed a couple of meetings in the afternoon.

Plus, there had been a lunch he was supposed to go to, hadn't there? With his dad, his brothers Ash and Matt and a couple of BravoCorp's biggest investors. He knew he shouldn't have blown that off. His assistant, Georgia, had probably spent the day going nuts, calling him over and over, wondering where the hell he'd gotten off to. He should have called her when he decided to take Mary to the hospital.

And he needed to stop putting off calling his dad. Davis was probably past being annoyed with him and starting to get worried. He didn't want that.

But then he thought about Mary. And Ginny.

And somehow all that crap that added up to his real life…? So what about that?

Later. For all of it.

He was still hungry, so he got another sandwich, more coffee and a piece of chocolate cake. That time he ate slowly, letting Mary have all the time she needed, to talk to Ida, to eat her own dinner.

Almost an hour had gone by when he poked his head back in the door of her room. She'd switched off the lamp by the bed. Only the dim recessed light in the ceiling, turned down low, bathed the room in a dim glow. The remains of her meal waited on the swinging bed tray, which she'd pushed to the side. She seemed to be sleeping, her head turned to the far wall. He couldn't see the baby, but figured she must be in the bassinet on the other side of the bed.

He started to duck back out again, thinking how it was

time, after all, for him to go. He could slip away without disturbing either of them, and get in touch in the morning, to make sure she was doing okay.

But Mary turned her head with a sigh and saw him, her eyes half-open, a slow smile curving her soft mouth. She whispered his name. "Gabe…" And she held out the hand without the IV hooked into the back of it.

His heart strangely lighter, he slipped into the dim room and let the door shut silently behind him.

Chapter Five

After he put her dinner tray outside the door, Gabe returned to Mary, took the hand she offered and sat in the chair. They were quiet for several minutes, just being there, together, in the dark. He could hear Ginny's breathing, even and shallow, from the bassinet across the bed.

"She's sleeping," Mary whispered, and squeezed his hand. He was thinking that she was bound to drift off to sleep herself in a minute or two. Then he would go.

But instead of closing her eyes, she whispered, "Poor Ida. She's all upset she wasn't here. She said Helga took a turn for the worse. Ida had to rush her to the hospital—and in the confusion, she left her cell at Helga's house."

Funny, but by then, he'd started to feel as if he knew Mary's mother-in-law—and her sister, Helga White, too. "Is Helga okay?"

"She's better, Ida said."

He realized he didn't even know what illness Helga suffered from. "What's going on with Helga?"

"She has heart problems. Low blood pressure and congestive heart failure. This time, her heartbeat slowed and almost stopped. They got her stabilized at the hospital. But now they're talking about a pacemaker. She'll be hospitalized for the next several days."

"So what will Ida do—I mean, now that Ginny's here?"

"She says she can get her other sister, Johanna, to fly up from Arizona and take over with Helga. Ida says they agreed, she and her sisters, that she would have to be here when the baby came. Poor Ida…" Mary chuckled, low. "She feels so bad she wasn't here for me—and plus, there's the disappointment. She wanted so much to see her grandchild born. This was a once-in-a-lifetime deal for her. Rowdy was her only child."

"That's rough."

She shrugged. "Oh, she'll get over it—the minute she gets her arms around Ginny."

Ginny. So Mary was calling the baby Ginny, too. He supposed it was a logical choice as a nickname for Virginia. Maybe it had even been the name Mary's mother went by. Still, for some crazy reason, it pleased him to no end that he had called her Ginny first, and that Mary thought of her as Ginny, too.

Gabe shook his head. Was he losing it or what?

Mary was watching him. "What?"

As if he would ever cop to getting all warm and fuzzy because they both called her baby Ginny. "Nothing. So Ida's coming back to look after you, huh?"

She nodded. "It might be a few days until she and her sisters get things worked out and she can come home. And

Dr. Breitmann said they'll probably release me from the hospital tomorrow afternoon, if there are no complications. So in the meantime, until she gets here, Ida insists I'm supposed to get a doula to stay out at the house with us. Ida will foot the bill."

"Okay, I'll bite. What's a doula?"

"Kind of a combination housekeeper, nanny and nurse."

"Where do you find one?"

"Ida will make some calls and get back to me with some numbers."

"Well, all right then. You'll have a doula."

Her eyes were shining. "So everything will work out— oh, and I told Ida all about you."

He faked a scowl. "All about me…like what?"

"Like how you came over to try and get me to sell the Lazy H and ended up driving me to the hospital and sticking with me right through to the end. She says you're a hero and she can't wait to meet you—but to warn you that if you think I'll sell that raggedy stretch of sagebrush and boulders Rowdy left me just because you came to my rescue in my hour of need, you've got another think coming."

Ida's warning didn't surprise him. "She loves the ranch, too, huh?"

"Uh-uh. She hates it. It belonged to her husband and he made her live there when she wanted a house in town. He left it to Rowdy, knowing that if Ida got her hands on it, she'd sell it in a heartbeat."

He couldn't help thinking that maybe Ida was the one he should approach with BravoCorp's offer. If he convinced her she needed to put the pressure on Mary for Mary's own good, and Ginny's, too…

But Mary was one step ahead of him. "I see that gleam

in your eye, Gabe Bravo. Don't even think about it. Ida knows I love the ranch. And more than anything, she wants me to be happy. You try to get her to put pressure on me, she'll tell you you're on your own with that and send you on your way."

"She doesn't sound like your average mother-in-law."

She slid him a sideways glance. "You got something against mothers-in-law?"

"Not in the least. I've never even had one."

She made a soft snorting sound. "Bachelor to the core. I knew it."

"And damn proud of it—so you're crazy about your mother-in-law, huh?"

"I am. Ida's the best there is. No joke. Plus, she's how I met Rowdy. I moved down from Dallas and went to work at the store. I'd always had this fantasy about living in the Hill Country." Between San Antonio and Austin, right in the geographical heart of Texas, the Hill Country was a lot of folks' idea of country living at its best. "I guess you could say I was finally living my dream," Mary went on. "And Ida was so kind to me. I was just…I don't know, so attached to her from the beginning. I'd lost my mom about a year before. Ida didn't take her place, exactly. But she sure helped fill the empty space Mom left when she died."

Gabe thought about that nice, thick dossier he had on Mary, worked up by the best private investigators Bravo-Corp's money could buy. He knew that she'd been raised by a single mom, in Arlington, a good-sized city about ten miles east of Fort Worth. He knew the small college she'd gone to and when she'd moved to Wulf Creek and met her husband. Still, he asked her, "What about your dad?"

She shook her head, kind of slow and sad. "He left us

when I was two. I don't even remember him. It was always just me and Mom. She was so…smart and loving and always there for me, you know? I hardly knew what to do with myself when I lost her. She was a schoolteacher."

Mary spoke so openly about what must have been damn tough for her and her mom. And that had him feeling like a complete jerk, to be hiding the ball like this, asking her for personal information he already had. He busted himself. "Your mom taught primary grades, right?"

She caught on instantly. He watched her soft eyes grow guarded as awareness dawned. He found himself thinking, as he had when he first met her, that she was too quick by half.

In a whisper, she accused him. "You've had people looking into my past."

"Yeah." He met her gaze directly. "It's what I do, Mary. You know that."

"Why ask me if you already know it all?" She pulled her hand from his.

He took it back again, turned it over, ran his finger along the crease at the tender center of her palm. "Because this isn't about business, Mary. This is strictly personal. I want to know about you. I want you to *tell* me about you."

She eased her hand from his a second time. At that point, what could he do but let it go? While he'd been down in the cafeteria, she must have cleaned up a little. She smelled faintly of lemons again. And she'd run a comb through her hair. It fell smoothly to her shoulders, still in need of a shampoo and a good cut, but no longer matted and stringy with sweat. She speared her fingers back through the chestnut strands. "What time is it?" Before he could answer, she glanced up at the round clock on the wall across from the bed. "Eight-thirty." Finally, she looked at him again. "You've been so terrific. I don't know how I would have gotten through this without you…"

He got the message. "You want me to go."

"Well, I mean, it doesn't seem right. You've been here all day. I'm sure you have all kinds of…things to catch up on."

"Mary. I saw your baby born. I think we're pretty much past all the polite-sounding noises. Say what you mean."

"Okay. Thank you. For everything…."

"You're angry, because we've had detectives finding out about you."

She pressed her lips together. "Angry?"

"Just say it."

"But, Gabe, why should I be angry that you've been trying to find my weak points, nosing around in my life, looking for a way to get to me, to maneuver me into doing what I don't want to do?"

"All right." He spoke gruffly. "Yeah. It's rotten that we had our investigators nosing around in your private business. What can I say about that? Except I didn't even know you then."

Her face softened. "Just business, right?"

He shrugged. "That's right."

"And really, when I think about it, it's only what I should have expected. But it does remind me…"

"Of what?"

"That the crisis is over. You *have* been wonderful, Gabe. I can't thank you enough."

"But?"

"It's time for you to go."

That hurt, her sending him packing. Even if she did

happen to be right. It *was* time for him to leave. It was past time. But that didn't make it hurt any less.

Which made him, what? An idiot. A complete fool. A sentimental schmuck. All of the above.

"Well, all right." He kept it light, rising, bending over her, kissing her forehead, whispering, "Sleep well."

She stopped him as he pulled open the door to the hallway. "Gabe?"

"Yeah?" Hope burned in his chest, embarrassing the hell out of him. But she only gave him a smile and a shy little wave.

Outside, it was night. Cool and cloudless. He got behind the wheel of the SUV and then, before he started the engine, he did what he should have done hours ago: called his dad.

Davis Bravo was freaked. "Gabe." He swore. "You scared ten years off my life."

Gabe felt a stab of guilt, then. A few months before, his older brother's plane had gone down in the Sierras. Ash had survived the crash, but it had been more than a week before they found him. Gabe probably should have considered that getting out of touch for a day when he was supposed to be at work would have his father worried sick.

His dad demanded, "Where in God's name are you?"

"Wulf City. And I'm fine. Sorry, Dad. I'm really sorry."

"Your mother was about ready to call in the FBI *and* the Texas Rangers."

"Seriously. I'm safe and sound and you can call off the dogs. Tell Mom I love her, I'm not injured, bleeding or otherwise in trouble, and I'm less than thirty-five miles from home."

A silence on the line, and then, "All right. As long as you're okay." Again, Gabe reassured his father that he was fine. Davis must have believed him, because he got down to business after that. "What happened with the Hofstetter woman?"

So Gabe laid it all out for him, that he'd just finished giving his pitch when Mary had started having contractions, and he'd taken her to the hospital—and ended up staying through the birth, since she was all on her own. "I just now left her," he finished, "a few minutes ago, with her newborn baby girl in the bassinet beside her."

Another silence, then Davis let out a low laugh. "I have to hand it to you, son. You have got the touch. Now you and the Hofstetter widow are best friends, am I right?"

Gabe answered flatly. "We *are* friends, as a matter of fact."

"And she's agreed to sell that ranch, right?"

"Wrong."

"But she will. You'll talk her into it, show her the light."

"You know, Dad…"

"What?"

"She's firm on not selling. I always hate admitting failure. But this time, I have to tell you, it's beyond my talents to change her mind."

Davis sputtered. "What the hell?"

"You heard me. She doesn't want to sell."

His dad made a scoffing sound. "As if that's news. Come on. What do you think we sent you in for?"

Gabe took that as a rhetorical question and kept his mouth shut.

His father provided the answer anyway, in an insulting sing-song. "Because she doesn't want to sell." Davis paused, but he wasn't done. "And don't give me the limp leg on this. You're going to change her mind for her, just like you always do."

Gabe suppressed a sigh. "You got a whole lot of faith in me, Dad."

"You bet I do. You've proved to me over and over that my faith is justified. Now, all I want is for you to prove it one more time."

Gabe felt a weariness then, deep in his bones. When Davis Bravo wanted something, the word "no" disappeared from his vocabulary. "I'm tired, Dad. Heading home. Good night."

"Gabe. Gabe, I'm not finished talking to—"

"Gotta go." Gabe disconnected and tossed the Black-Berry onto the seat beside him. He started up the Escalade and was just pulling out of the parking lot when he remembered that Mary had horses and goats. And chickens, too. And there was also that scraggly brown dog. Was anybody looking after them?

He decided he might as well go ahead and check on things at the Lazy H. Feed the stock and pet the damn dog. No big deal. It was between there and home. Hardly out of his way at all.

There was a battered green pickup in the backyard when Gabe drove around to the rear of Mary's house. And a light on in the barn. Evidently, Mary had already called someone to look after the stock.

Still, Gabe got out of the Escalade quietly and approached the lit-up barn with caution. Inside, he found a skinny old man in overalls coming in from what Gabe assumed was the horse paddock. The old guy had a bucket in either hand and Mary's brown dog at his heels. The dog whined and came straight for Gabe, dropping to her haunches, looking up at him hopefully. Gabe knelt to give her a little attention. He petted her head and scratched her around the ruff of her neck.

The old guy squinted at him. "Who's that there?"

Gabe knew harmless when he saw it. He rose and stepped forward, his hand outstretched. "I'm Gabe. A friend of Mary's."

The old man dropped a bucket so they could shake. "Garland Hadley, friend of the family. I got me a small spread northwest of here. Rowdy's dad and me, we went way back."

"Mary give you a call?"

"Yep. Said she had her a baby girl named Virginia Mae and would I mind lookin' after the animals." The old guy dropped the other bucket, swiped off his straw hat and scratched the few wiry-looking hairs on the top of his head. "Great news, 'bout that baby. Shame Rowdy didn't live to see her." He looked Gabe up and down. "You knew Rowdy?"

"Never had the pleasure."

"A fine man. I knew Rowdy since he was knee-high to a gnat." He shook his head and hit his hat against his thigh. "Cryin' shame he's gone."

"Yes, it is." It seemed the right thing to say. "Anything I can help you with here?"

"Naw. Got it handled. You know when Mary's coming home?"

"Tomorrow afternoon, I think."

"I'll look in on her when she gets back, look after the livestock for the next few days."

"I know she'll appreciate that."

"I heard Ida's in Missouri. Mary got someone to drive her home?" The old man asked the question and it all came clear to Gabe.

"Yeah. I'm taking care of that."

Garland nodded and slid his hat back on. "You'll be needin' that car seat she bought. I got a key to the house. Come on. I'll get it for you."

Mary woke in the middle of the night and wondered where she was.

And then it all came flooding back: the hospital. She was at Wulf City Memorial.

And Ginny. She'd had Ginny.

She rolled her head to the other side, slowly, almost fearing that when she looked, she'd find only emptiness in the space where Ginny's bassinet was supposed to be. She'd learn it had all been a dream.

But no. No dream. Real.

Ginny lay on her back, sleeping so peacefully, making darling little sucking motions with her tiny mouth. Mary's arms ached to hold her close. But no, better to let her get her sleep. The poor sweetie needed it, after what she'd been through. Toughest job in the world, being born. Mary grinned to think of it. Easy enough to grin now that all the hard work was done.

Gabe.

She thought his name and she felt…lonely. She missed him. Which was downright crazy, if you considered it. She hardly knew him. He was only a slick operator, a rich guy from a world she didn't understand, sent in to smooth-talk her into signing over her ranch.

"No…" She whispered the denial to the silent, darkened room.

He wasn't only that. He was *more.* He had been good to her. Kind and helpful and *there,* ready and able to do what had to be done when she needed him, needed a friend. Even when she'd tried to get rid of him back at the house, to tell him she would manage by herself, he wouldn't leave her to find a way to the hospital on her own.

After everything he'd been through for her and Ginny's sake, she shouldn't have sent him off like that in the end, so abruptly. Just because he'd let slip that he knew more about her than he should—in fact, now she thought it over some, she couldn't see him messing up like that. Uh-uh. He was too good at what he did. Which meant he'd done it on purpose.

Why?

Mary smiled into the darkness. To get straight with her. Because a man needed to be straight with his friends.

Her smile faded and her brows drew together. She had a self-righteous streak, and she knew it. She shouldn't have jumped right into blaming him that way.

Mary reached for her cell on the table by the bed. She would call him, right now, and tell him she was sorry, tell him….

Too bad she didn't have his number. He'd given her that card when she answered the door, and she'd stuck it in the back pocket of her jeans—which she'd left on the floor of her bathroom after her water broke.

Feeling strangely bereft, she set the phone down and leaned back on the pillows and told herself it was no big deal. She would be home by tomorrow afternoon. She'd call him then.

Which was another problem. She still needed to get someone to collect Ginny's car seat from the house and come get her tomorrow.

Tomorrow, she thought as she closed her eyes. She'd

arrange for Donna Lynn or Garland to take her home. And when she got there, the first thing she would do—even before she called the editor of *Ranch Life* to explain why she'd missed her deadline—was to call Gabe and thank him again for being the best unexpected friend any girl ever had.

Ginny started fussing. Mary took her from the bassinet and put her to the breast, laughing a little at the way she latched right on and sucked for all she was worth. Mary knew from all the reading she'd done that her nipples would be seriously sore in the next day or two. Right then, though, all she could think about was the darling child in her arms. She might have been born a few weeks early, but she was none the weaker for it. Virginia Mae Hofstetter was going to thrive and grow.

Oh, if only Rowdy could see her…

Mary felt the hot tears scald her cheeks where she'd been laughing just a moment earlier. Oh, she was just a tangled mess of emotion, all right. But that was to be expected, too. When you had a baby, hormones had a field day with your heart.

Mary smiled through her tears and whispered, "Rowdy, we made it through." She stroked the feathery wisps of hair on Ginny's little head. "She will know you, I swear it to you. She will know that you loved her without ever knowing her. That you wanted her so much, that you never would have left her by your own choice. This is one lucky girl, here. To be able to call a man as fine as you her daddy…"

In a while, Mary switched her baby to the other side. She sang to Ginny, so softly, an Irish song about a fishmonger's daughter that her mother used to sing to her. Finally, Ginny heaved a huge sigh for such a small person and let go of Mary's nipple. She was already asleep again. Mary held her for a while, just loving the feel of her.

And then she lifted her to her shoulder and patted her tiny back. Ginny let out a hearty-sounding burp, never even waking. Gently, so carefully, Mary laid her back in the bassinet. Then she plumped her pillow and closed her eyes and drifted off to sleep again.

The next time she woke, it was almost 2:00 a.m. She needed to pee, so she put the bed rail down and got up, with considerable effort. They'd taken away her IV a few hours back and she kind of missed it. The pole had been good to lean on as she shuffled along. Slowly, groaning more than once at the stiffness in every single part of her body, she made it into the bathroom and did what she needed to do.

Then she washed her hands and shuffled out into the main room again. She paused at the bedside, thinking how much it was going to hurt to lift up her leg and hoist herself onto the mattress again.

Maybe a little stroll in the corridor outside her room first. The nurses had said she should get up and walk as soon as she felt she could handle it, that it would help to "get things moving," meaning her bowels.

Getting things moving aside, Mary thought, as she frowned at the bed, anything would be easier than climbing back up there. Maybe if she walked a little, her aching muscles would loosen up.

Since the thin hospital gown wasn't something she wanted to walk the hallways in, she took the robe she'd brought from home off the end of the bed. With slow care—her body was so sore and achy even the simplest actions seemed to take forever—she pulled on the robe and belted it.

And then, at last, she set out. Such a big adventure—a walk down the hospital hallway. She shuffled over to the door, pulled it open and blinked against the bright glare of the lights out there.

A passing orderly paused to grant her a big smile, his teeth so white and straight in his dark face. "Way to go, Mary. The more you walk, the faster you're out of here."

She gave him a game thumbs-up.

He nodded his approval. "And if you're looking for your husband, he's right over there."

"My...?"

"Right there."

Her gaze followed where he pointed. Gabe was conked out in a chair against the wall several yards down the hallway.

Tenderness flooded through her at the sight of him. She felt the soft smile as it curved her lips. He had his head braced on his hand, his neck bent at a really painful-looking angle. He'd need a chiropractor when he woke up, the poor man.

The orderly stepped closer. "Between you and me, Mary?"

"Hmm?"

"He looks pretty uncomfortable."

"He sure does."

"He said he didn't want to wake you."

"He's, um, thoughtful that way."

"You should take him in your room with you. No one's going to care if he stretches out on that empty bed in there."

"You think?"

"Go on. Give the poor man a bed to sleep in." The orderly strolled off down the hall.

Mary hovered there, at the door to her room, staring at Gabe as he slept. How could it be she'd met him just yesterday? When she looked at him now, she felt the same deep, abiding fondness a person feels for someone she's known since grade school.

Her mom used to say that a faithful friend was a gift to treasure. Gabe didn't seem the faithful type, or he hadn't at first. But already, in the space of mere hours, he'd proved himself one of the best friends she'd ever known.

A gift to treasure, yes he was.

Mary started toward him, wincing as she went, one slow step at a time.

Chapter Six

Gabe smelled lemons and heard Mary calling his name. He muttered, "S'okay, Mary. Li'l nap…" and tried to sink back into sleep again.

But Mary wouldn't shut up. "Gabe. Come on." She was shaking his shoulder, whispering in his ear. "Wake up…"

He opened one eye. "Ugh. What?" He rubbed the back of his neck. A hard chair in a hospital corridor wasn't the most comfortable place to sleep.

She was bent close, her hair brushing his cheek. As he peered at her blearily, she straightened, groaning at the effort it took, and put her fists on her hips. She stared down at him, shaking her head.

At least she didn't look mad. "I guess there's no need to ask you what you're doing here."

"Well, see, it's like this." He rubbed his neck some more. "I went by your place to check on the animals—"

"…and ran into Garland and the two of you talked about who would bring me home tomorrow."

He leaned back against the wall and let his eyes droop shut again. "Mary."

"What?"

"Let a man finish a damn sentence, why don't you?"

"Sorry."

"S'okay. Got your car seat in the Escalade…" He drifted back toward the comfort of sleep.

But she only shook his shoulder some more. "Gabe. Come on."

"C'mon, where?"

"The other bed. In my room. You can stretch out there, at least."

"S'all right. Really. I'm fine here."

"Gabe."

He felt her body's warmth and smelled her tart scent again. "Huh?" He gave in and opened his eyes.

Her face was maybe two inches from his. "Come *on*."

So he dragged himself upright and started for her room. A few steps along, he realized she wasn't following.

He glanced back. "Well. What's the holdup?" She blew out a put-upon breath and stiffly started shuffling toward him. He let her go on past, wanting to catch her arm as she went by and scoop her up into his arms, to carry her wherever she needed to go. "Hey, Mary."

She stopped to scowl over her shoulder. "What?"

"Need some help?"

"No, thank you," she said in that voice that brought to mind some old lady schoolteacher. "I'm managing just fine."

He grinned to himself and followed at her pace. She was something. She didn't let anything get her down.

In her darkened room, they were quiet in order not to wake Ginny. He tried to help her up into her bed.

"I said I would manage," she said in a crabby whisper.

He moved back. "Go for it."

So she did, with great effort. Once she was up there, she fussed with the pillow and wiggled around, getting out of her robe, which she tossed to the foot of the bed. Finally, with a hard sigh, she was still.

"So," he whispered, still standing where she'd left him when he'd tried to give her a hand up. "All settled?"

"Yes, I am."

"Well, all right." He tiptoed over to the other bed, eased off his boots and lay down with the rest of his clothes on, lacing his fingers behind his head. Sure beat sleeping in the hallway.

"Gabe?" she whispered through the darkness.

"Um?"

"I know I said it about a hundred times already, but thank you. For everything."

"For you, Mary, anything." He said it jokingly, but then he felt a sudden uncomfortable jolt deep down inside him as he realized he actually meant it.

There was something about her. Something solid and true. She made a man want to do what he could for her—partly because she seemed so determined to take care of herself. And partly because...

His mind veered away from the unnerving thought. He let it go.

She asked, "When you let it slip about nosing around in my life?"

"Yeah?"

"You made that slip on purpose, didn't you?"

He grinned at the shadowed ceiling overhead. That Mary. Nothing got by her. "It's not important."

"Oh, yeah. It is. You're an honorable man. Even if you think it's kind of corny to admit you are."

"Go to sleep, Mary."

A silence from her bed and then, "Yes, all right. Good night."

The baby woke at a little after four, fussing. The fussing built to a whine. And then a full-fledged wail.

Mary stirred in the other bed.

"What can I do?" Gabe asked.

"Not a thing," she said. "I'm on it."

He turned on his side and braced himself on an elbow and watched through the shadowed dark as she took Ginny in her arms and eased her hospital gown out of the way. The baby got right to work. And the room was quiet again, except for the sounds Ginny made as she ate.

"She's a hungry one," Gabe said.

Mary gazed down at her. Even through the shadows, he could see the faint curve of her adoring smile. "And it's not even milk yet."

"Huh?"

"It's called colostrum, and is produced before the milk comes down. It gives the baby the special nourishment she needs right after birth."

"Who knew?" he said wryly, thinking it was more information than he needed, but kind of interesting nonetheless.

After Ginny ate, Mary got up—slowly, as she'd been doing everything since the birth—and changed her and put her back in the bassinet. Gabe would have offered to help with that, but he knew she'd say no, which, really, was fine with him.

Once Ginny was back in her bed, Mary started walking again. Slowly. With a good deal of groaning. She made her way at a snail's pace to the bathroom. It seemed to Gabe, lying there in the dark, acutely aware of every move she made, that it took her forever to get there.

When she came out, it took her just as long to get back to the bed and up into it. Finally, she settled under the covers with a sigh. He lay there in the quiet dark for a while, listening to the baby's breathing, and then to Mary's, too, as she faded off to sleep, thinking how he felt content just to be lying there with Mary and her baby conked out a few feet away.

In the morning, the nurse came in while he was still asleep. He heard the soft sounds her crepe soles made on the linoleum floor.

He opened his eyes and the nurse smiled at him. "Mornin'," she said. "Going to be another sunny day." She unhooked Mary's chart from the foot of the bed and made a note on it.

Then she woke Mary and asked her some questions about how she was feeling. She took Mary's blood pressure and temperature and also checked the baby.

"Things are looking good," she said, and asked Mary if she had any questions.

"Just one. I need a shower. Can I have one?"

The nurse glanced at the chart again. "Sure. Breakfast should be here soon. How about after the meal? Will your husband help you, or do you want one of the ward clerks to come by?"

Mary sent him a glance he couldn't quite read. Maybe she was getting tired of them all calling him her husband.

Or maybe she wanted him to know that he would *not* be helping her with her shower.

Really, who knew what that look meant? He sure didn't.

She insisted, "I can do it myself, don't worry. I'm feeling so much better this morning."

"Well, fair enough, then." The nurse marked the chart again and left.

A few minutes later, they brought in breakfast. Someone had thought to order a tray for Gabe, too. Mary ate in bed, using the swinging tray as a table. He sat in one of the chairs, the food tray balanced on his knees.

Later, after she nursed the baby again, Mary wanted the shower the nurse had approved. By then it was after nine.

He offered to keep an eye on the baby while she was in the bathroom.

"No, it's okay. I can just leave the door open…"

He took the hint. "I've got a few calls to make anyway. Back in an hour or so?"

She looked sweetly relieved. "That would be real good."

He got a large coffee from the cafeteria, went outside and stood in the parking lot under the bright morning sun and called his assistant at the office.

He told her to clear his calendar for the rest of the day. "I won't be in the office until tomorrow."

Georgia was a prize. She didn't ask questions. "Will do, Gabe."

"Sorry about yesterday. Something big came up."

"It's all right. I managed." She gave him a brief rundown of the fires she'd put out in his absence.

He told her she was the best. Then they went over his schedule for the day and agreed on a tentative rearrangement. "Tell my father I'm taking a little time off for myself."

"That will be fun." She said it in a neutral tone.

But the cool remark forced him to admit it just wasn't fair to put a job like that on his assistant. "Never mind. I'll handle my father. You call the rest of them for me. If they ask, say I'm helping out a friend. If there's something you can't work out, call me here, on my cell, and I'll deal with it."

"Good enough."

Once he finished with Georgia, he called his dad and told him he'd be away from the office and out of contact for another day. "Georgia has it all handled," he added.

Davis was not reassured. "Okay, Gabe. What's going on? We've got the quarterly meeting today. And you're supposed to be handling the new project review. And then there's the formal update meeting of the Bravo River Group. There's—"

"Dad. I know my job."

"Something's going on with you," Davis growled. "I'm not happy about it."

Gabe almost laughed. As a rule, his father had sense enough to let his sons—and his two daughters—run their own lives. He trusted them to manage their separate responsibilities in or out of the family business without leaning over their shoulders or second-guessing their decisions.

But Davis could get controlling. Especially when he sensed that things weren't going the way he wanted them to go.

Davis said, "Is this about that Hofstetter woman?"

Gabe almost denied it, just on principle. But why? He wasn't some misbehaving kid who had to lie to his dad. "Yeah. She's on her own right now. She needs a helping hand."

There was a silence. Then his father said, "So you *are* still working on her. Good."

Gabe glanced up at the clear Texas sky and shook his head in exasperation, though there was no one to see but a few blackbirds on a telephone wire at the edge of the parking lot. "I'll say it once more, Dad. And that had better do it. No. I'm not working on her. I'm just helping her out."

Davis swore. "Your time is money. Hire her a nurse."

It was hopeless and Gabe knew it. His father was not going to understand—truth was, Gabe hardly understood. He only knew that helping Mary and Ginny was something he had to do. "Talk to you later, Dad." He pressed the disconnect button before Davis could bark more orders at him.

He had several other messages, both text and voice mail, so he went through them. He texted the ones he could and called the rest back, including Carly. He got her voice mail and left a brief message saying he'd try her later.

In the meantime, as he was dealing with yesterday's messages, more calls were coming in. He dealt with them, too.

Once he'd finally gotten on top of his calls, it was twenty past ten and he figured Mary was probably done with her shower. He went to the Escalade and got his overnight bag, packed the night before when he had gone back to his place after stopping at the ranch.

In the room, Mary, her hair clean and shiny after her shower, was making a few calls of her own. Gabe slipped into the bathroom, which was still steamy with the lemony scent of her. He used the shower and shaved.

When he emerged, she was looking very proud of herself. "I called my editor and got an extension on that article."

"Excellent." He sat on the bed beside her, thinking how good she smelled.

"I had a couple of projects due this week at other magazines. I got extensions for them, too."

"You've been busy, huh?"

She nodded. "And I talked to Donna Lynn. Since I'm going home in a few hours, she's just going to come and see me at the ranch, instead of trying to make time to drop in here."

"You call Ida?"

"I did. No news there. She's a little down, still not sure what day Johanna's coming. But she said it would be soon. I told her not to worry. And then held the phone down to Ginny and she made the cutest little cooing sound right on cue."

"Bet Ida loved that." He couldn't help noticing how her skin had a glow to it after her shower. He had to resist the urge to reach out and run the back of his hand down her soft, pink cheek.

Mary grinned. "She did love it. She laughed and said she felt better, just hearing her granddaughter's voice—oh. And I found a doula. The nanny agency Ida had me call said they'd have someone at the ranch at two. It's pretty short notice, they told me. Usually I would interview and everything…" She frowned to herself—and then brightened again. Her eyes, he realized, were not just brown. They had gold in them. And blue rims around the iris. She chattered on, "But I'm sure it will work out with her. And I figure we should be back home before two."

He got up and moved over to sit in the chair. It was safer that way. When he was close to her, he wanted to put his hands on her. Touching her had seemed perfectly acceptable yesterday, when she was having her baby. It had been like a different world then, a world with all the barriers down, where she needed his hand holding hers, his touch to calm and comfort her.

But now, this morning, with Ginny safely born, they were back in the real world where the old rules of conduct applied all over again. He was here to help, not get all up on her.

She was frowning at him from the bed. "Is something wrong?"

He played it off. "Not at all." And changed the subject. "Did Dr. Breitmann come by already then?"

Now she looked puzzled. "No. Why?"

"Well, he does have to release you before you can go home, right? Maybe telling the doula to be there at two was jumping the gun a little."

"No. I don't think so. I feel terrific—I mean, considering that I had a baby yesterday. As soon as Dr. Breitmann gets here, he'll be releasing me."

In the past twenty-four hours, Gabe had learned a lot about Mary. Things like how once she'd made up her mind, there was no point in arguing with her. Might as well just wait and see how it shook out.

Maybe it *would* turn out as she predicted. He'd no longer be needed by two that afternoon. He could head on back to his own life, end up dropping in at BravoCorp today after all, getting back on top of his workload.

That would be great, he tried to tell himself. That would be just great.

By eleven-thirty, when Dr. Breitmann had yet to show up, Mary was getting a little worried. She really did want to get out of the hospital that day, if possible. Partly because she would prefer to be in her own house, and partly because she did worry that her insurance might give her trouble about paying for another day.

Gabe didn't seem the least bit worried. He'd gotten his briefcase from the house when he picked up the car seat and he was on his laptop on and off, answering e-mails and such. When he'd get a call, he'd leave the room to answer it, ever thoughtful not to disturb her or the baby. She stared at his golden-brown head, bent over his PDA thingy, thumbs flying as he replied to a text message, and she smiled to herself.

What a great guy he'd turned out to be, at her side all yesterday and today, willing to hang around waiting to take her home.

If she ever got to *go* home. At this rate, she was beginning to wonder.

"Gabe?"

He looked from his laptop with an absent-minded smile. "Hmm?"

"You think maybe I should call that nanny agency back, tell them to send the doula later?"

He shrugged. "Up to you."

"Maybe I'll just call Dr. Breitmann's office and see what the holdup is."

"Up to you," he said again, kind of absently, already back on that text message he was writing, little keys clicking away.

So she called Dr. Breitmann's office and they said he was delivering a baby. But it was looking like he might make it in to see her by one. Mary thanked the receptionist and hung up.

And then she worried. If he came at one, would that be

time, with checking out and everything, to get to the house before two?

Gabe glanced up from his PDA again. "What's the matter?"

What? *Now* he was interested? "Nothing's the matter. I don't know what you mean."

"Come on. You're huffing and puffing, flopping around in that bed like you can't wait to get out of it."

"Well, I *can't* wait. I'm sick of just lying here, wondering when my doctor's finally going to show up."

"So go for a walk down to the nurses' station and back. Walking's supposed to be good for you, isn't it?"

How could someone so helpful and wonderful be so annoying? She made a shooing movement with her fingers. "Just…write another text message and stop telling me what to do."

Gabe shook his head and did just that.

And by then she'd decided that the helper coming at two really was cutting it too close. She called the agency and told them not to send the doula until four. That should be plenty of time.

They ate lunch mostly in silence, except for when his PDA vibrated and he went out to answer it.

When he came back in, she sourly suggested, "I'm surprised you don't have one of those phones that hook over your ear. Doesn't everybody in the big-time business world have a 'hands-free' now?"

"I don't like them," he said, and took another bite of soupy-looking Swiss steak.

It wasn't important. She should have left it alone. But she was getting fed up with waiting for Dr. Breitmann and poor Gabe was the only one there to torture. "Why not?"

He set down his fork. "You really want to know?"

She didn't care in the least. "Yeah. I do."

"When you use them, you look like you're talking to yourself. That turns people off. It's my job *not* to turn people off."

"You mean, while you're making them an offer they can't refuse?"

He picked up his fork again. "Mary. Be quiet and eat your lunch."

She opened her mouth to say something really angry and vile. But sanity returned at the last possible second. She shut up and let a huffy glare suffice for a reply.

Yes, she knew she was acting like a spoiled brat. She really did have to watch it or she'd say something unforgivable to Gabe who in no way deserved such crappy treatment. If only Dr. Breitmann would come and tell her she was doing fine and she could go.

But then what if he said she had to stay?

No. Why would he do that? She felt pretty good, physically, considering. But her whole body still hurt. When she tried to walk, she shuffled along with all the spunk and agility of a very old, sick woman. And she had cramping. And there was still some bleeding. Both the cramps and the bleeding were normal. She knew that. So were the stiffness and the other pains.

Still, what if there was something wrong? Would she be stuck here while they worked her over some more, at Lord knew how many hard-earned dollars a day?

By the time they'd finished their silent lunch, Gabe must have noticed how stressed she was getting. He tried to kid her out of it. "You're going to lose those molars if you don't stop grinding them."

She leveled a glare on him. "Do not get cute with me. Not now."

He arranged his incredibly handsome face into an expression of great seriousness. "Mary. I give up. Wear your molars down. Grunt and groan and make ugly faces. You're on your own with it. I won't say another word to try and cheer you up."

"Good. See that you don't."

Dr. Breitmann finally showed up at one-thirty. Gabe, probably only too happy to get away from her and her terrible attitude, left them alone for the exam.

Twenty minutes later, after the doctor left, Gabe tapped on the door. Mary called to him to come in.

He stuck his head in. "Well?"

She confessed, softly, "I'm sorry. I know I've been snippy."

"That's putting it mildly."

"You're right. I've been just awful. And I'm sorry. Truly."

"It's okay. You just had a baby. You're entitled."

"No, I'm not. But the good news is it's safe to come in now. I'm fine. The baby's fine. And we get to go home."

Mary sat in the backseat with Ginny when Gabe drove them home.

She stared out the window at the rolling, dry land and the wide Texas sky where a hawk wheeled, high up, seeking prey, and tried not to think that in a couple of hours, he would be gone. She reminded herself that she'd have a helper until Ida got back, a woman trained to take care of new mothers and their babies. She and the doula would get along great.

And Gabe had done more than she ever would or could have asked of him. Done it willingly. Eagerly, even. With a whole bunch of patience and a sense of humor to boot.

Now she was going to need to let him go. And she would. She would thank him for the hundredth time and smile as he went out the door.

In no time, he was pulling to a stop in front of her house. Brownie ran out to greet them, sitting down like a good dog, her tongue hanging out as she panted with happiness.

It took a while to get the baby and the car seat and all the other stuff inside. Then Gabe asked where the baby's room was and she told him it was upstairs.

He gave her a look. "Maybe for a few weeks you should just move her bed down here, in your room, with you."

"Yes. That's exactly what I'd planned to do. I was going to take care of that a week or so before the baby was due…"

"Tell me what you need," he said. "I'll bring it down for you."

"Oh, no. Really. You've done way too much already. The doula can take care of it when she gets here."

"Mary." He waited until he was sure she was listening. Then he repeated, "Tell me what you need from up there."

She gave in and told him. He brought it all down: the bassinet and changing table, along with stacks of receiving blankets and onesies—most all of the stuff Mary had collected for Ginny's layette. They set up a baby station in a corner of the master bedroom and put the bassinet on the far side of the bed, in easy reach at night.

By the time they had it all properly arranged, it was quarter after four with no sign of the doula.

"Give her fifteen more minutes," Gabe suggested. "Then I guess you'd better call."

Mary blew out a breath. "All right—and really, there's no reason you have to stay until—"

He put up a hand. "Stop."

"But you don't have to—"

"I'm not leaving you alone."

"But I'm—"

"Give it up. It's out of the question. I don't want to hear any more about it."

So they waited. No doula. At four-thirty, Mary called. The agency said they'd been just about to call *her*. The woman they'd sent had checked in a few minutes before to say she had a family emergency and wouldn't be available that day or the next after all. They had no one else they could send on such short notice. But if she still needed someone on Thursday, they should be able to help her then.

Mary said she'd get back to them. And then she got out the phone book and started making calls. It took over an hour, but she finally found a domestic agency that said they could send someone the next morning.

When she hung up, Gabe was waiting, one eyebrow raised. "A domestic agency? So you're just getting a maid?"

"No, I'm getting a 'home care specialist.' She'll be here tomorrow at nine, to do light housekeeping and help with the baby."

"Well, good," he said. "I can call the office and tell them I'll be in a couple of hours late tomorrow. No biggie."

Her heart lifted at the thought. He wouldn't go, after all. But no. It just wasn't fair to him. "Oh, Gabe. I couldn't…"

"Sure you can. It's nothing. I'll stay."

"I could…ask Donna Lynn. And if she can't do it, I know a couple of other friends in Wulf City who might be willing. Someone will be able to come, I know it."

"Forget it. I'm here. I know the drill. You're used to having me around."

Oh, and she was! More than she should have let herself be. She should just put her foot down on this, now.

But he took the phone from her and set it on the table. And she let him.

"Just till the morning, then," she said, trying to sound firm and ending up sounding strangely breathless.

"That's right. Till the home care specialist arrives."

Chapter Seven

That evening, Gabe met Donna Lynn, the clerk from Hofstetter Hardware.

He also met three other women, a neighbor and two of Mary's girlfriends from Wulf City. They all came bearing casseroles, enough food to feed a small army, so Mary wouldn't have to worry about cooking for the next few days.

The women were nice. They did the usual things women do—talked baby talk to Ginny and said she was "just gorgeous. The prettiest little girl in Texas," and took turns holding her, each one sighing and going on about how tiny she was, and how sweet.

They treated him politely and said how great it was that he was there to help when Mary needed a friend. Mary joked that he'd come to buy her ranch—and when she wouldn't sell, he'd stayed to help her have her baby. If they thought it odd that a man she'd only met the day before was playing nursemaid to Mary and her newborn, they never let on.

Donna Lynn, a pretty, plump fifty-something with big hair and long red nails, did tease him. She said she'd seen pictures of him in *San Antonio Living* magazine, some ball or event he'd attended. "I mean to tell you, Gabe. You look mighty fine in a tux."

Mary sent him a warm smile. "And he's got the patience of a saint, too. I'm a fortunate woman that he showed up when he did."

If he'd been sitting next to her at that moment, he might have pulled her close and kissed her without thinking twice about it. But he wasn't. He stood across the room. Which was a lucky thing. He wasn't there in Mary's house to kiss her, and he needed to keep that fact clearly in mind.

Later, when all the women had left, Garland came by to feed the livestock. Mary asked the old guy in to see the baby and he let her talk him into eating some of the food her friends had brought.

When he went back out to the barn, Gabe went with him to help out. Together they tended the scruffy chickens, the two old horses and that family of ornery Nubian goats.

By the time Garland left, it was after nine. And dark out, the sky so clear that even the quarter moon gave enough light to see by. In fact, Gabe thought, as he paused on the back deck, Mary's spread looked pretty good by moonlight. You couldn't see how badly the barn needed paint and a new roof, or the way the ironwork posts that held up the raggedy patio cover were rusting.

It was nice. Quiet. Gabe gave into the temptation to sit for a few minutes and enjoy the night air. He dropped into a plastic chair, thinking how he wouldn't mind at all if Mary joined him.

And then he heard the storm door creak.

Sure enough. "Gabe?"

"Right here." He turned in the chair and saw her standing in the open door to the kitchen, holding the storm door wide, the light from inside making a halo around her hair. "What do you need?"

"Not a thing."

Still, he made a move to rise.

"Just sit back down," she insisted. And then she asked, kind of hesitantly, "Mind if I sit with you?"

The other plastic chair scraped the patio's concrete floor as he pulled it closer to his. "Come on."

So she came out, her dog at her heels, and sat next to him, wincing a little as she lowered herself into the chair. The dog walked in a circle and lay down at her feet. Mary wrapped the lightweight zip-front hoodie she wore a little tighter around her. They stared at the sky together.

"Nice night," she said.

"Yeah. Ginny…?"

"Sleeping." Mary tipped her head toward the house. "And the bedroom window's right there. I left it open a crack, so I'll hear her if she starts crying." Another silence between them. The good kind of silence. The kind friends can share, easy and comfortable.

After a while, she spoke again. "Talk to me, Gabe."

He laughed low. "Well, all right. What do you want to hear?"

"I'm thinking that since you already had detectives find out all there is to know about me, it's only fair you should tell me a little about you."

He shrugged. "I'm thirty-two. Got a business degree from UT and a law degree from Baylor. Never been married and no serious entanglements."

She sent him a grin. "You say that with such pride."

"I like the single life."

"Your mom and dad?"

"My mom's name's Aleta. Randall was her maiden name. It's an old San Antonio family."

"You love your mom. I can hear it in your voice. That's good. A man *should* love his mom."

"What's not to love? She had nine kids and somehow she manages to make each one of us feel like we're the favorite. She's a kind woman—good at heart, you know? And smart. With a great sense of humor. Bluebonnet eyes, my dad always says. And still good-looking, even now, after all these years and all those kids."

"And your dad?"

Gabe thought about his father for a moment. "Tough," he said finally. "My dad is tough. And ambitious. A survivor. He was the oldest of seven sons."

"And then he turned right around and had seven sons of his own."

"That's right. But all my uncles got the hell out as soon as they were old enough to take care of themselves, just to get away from my grandpa James. My dad's the only one who hung around, the only one tough enough, he always claims. He used Grandpa's money to make more money and when Grandpa died, my dad was his only heir."

"Would you say your dad married 'up'?"

"Yeah. Not that he didn't have money and power already. My grandfather did pretty well for himself. He started with nothing, came here from Wyoming and won

Bravo Ridge on a bet. That was in the early fifties. Then they found oil on the ranch. So Grandpa did all right and my dad took over from him. But my mom's family was wealthier than the Bravos when she married my dad. And the Randalls go way back in San Antonio, since before statehood."

She stared out at the night. And then she turned to him. "The first guy you sent out here to talk me into selling?"

"What about him?"

"When he told me he represented BravoCorp and the Bravo family, I thought about the Bravo Baby. You ever heard that old story?"

He nodded. Everyone remembered the Bravo Baby. Child of a powerful Southern California family, he was almost as famous as the Lindbergh baby. The Bravo Baby had been kidnapped, snatched in the middle of the night from his crib. His family paid a fortune in diamonds to ransom him back. The kidnapper took the money but never returned the baby. The world thought the child must be dead, but he'd lived. He grew up in Oklahoma City with no idea who he really was. They finally found him thirty years later—it turned out he'd been kidnapped by his own uncle, the notorious polygamist Blake Bravo.

Gabe confessed, "Blake Bravo was my father's cousin."

She gaped at him. "Get outta town."

"Seriously. Christmas before last, I went to a big family reunion in Vegas. I met a bunch of Blake's grown children. *And* the grown-up Bravo Baby. He's a PI in Oklahoma City now, married to a woman who lived next door to him when he was a kid."

"Before he had any idea who he really was, you mean?"

"That's right."

She looked at the stars again. "It's a dinky little world, when you come right down to it."

"Guess so."

"And I want to know more about your mom and dad…"

"Like what?"

"Still together?"

"They are. It's a solid marriage. Sometimes I wonder why she puts up with him."

"Maybe she loves him."

He turned to meet her eyes in the moonlight. "Yeah. She does. And he loves her. Married more than thirty years and still crazy for each other. That's pretty good, I think."

"In this day and age? That's a lot better than just pretty good." She smiled out at the night. A dreamy sort of smile. "You're lucky, to have grown up with two parents who love each other. My mom was the best. But I wanted a dad so bad." A sad laugh escaped her. "I used to pray that he'd come back to us. Truly. Down on my knees at the side of my bed every night, praying to the good Lord to bring my daddy back to me. And then, as I grew up, I got a little cynical, I guess. About men. And marriage. I couldn't see what all the hoorah was about." She was quiet, staring up at the far-away stars. "And then I met Rowdy." She shook her head, slowly, and sighed. "There was just…something about that man. He was so good and kind and sweet. A truly *fine* man. I loved him and I married him. And even though I lost him way too soon, I'm so glad I knew him, if only for a little while…."

He should have kept his mouth shut. But he didn't. "He died in a riding accident?"

She nodded. "He went out to fix a section of fence. Hours later, his old mare, Sagebrush, wandered back without him. We found him in the middle of the night. Something must have spooked the horse. He took a fall. Hit his head and broke his neck. Died instantly, they told me…."

Gabe said nothing as Mary stared out into the night, long gone in private memories of a man he'd never met, a single tear sliding over her cheek, shining in the moonlight.

Strange emotions welled inside him. He sat very still, resisting the ugly urge to say something hurtful, something cruel—anything to wipe that look of longing off her face.

Jealous. I'm jealous.

He thought it and instantly tried to deny it.

But he couldn't. There was no denying it. He was jealous of a dead man. A dead man who had owned a hundred and twenty overgrown acres and a tumbledown shack, yet had somehow managed to lay claim to the heart of a woman like Mary.

He wondered, feeling sick to the core, what in hell was happening to him. He'd never been the jealous type.

From inside the house, they both heard the faint cry.

"I'll get her." He started to stand.

But Mary reached across and put her hand on his arm. Her touch seemed to burn him, to brand him inside his skin.

Her voice came to him. "You stay put." She sounded relaxed, no hint of tension. "Enjoy the evening." He realized she didn't have a clue what was going on inside him. "I'll see to her." And she pushed herself upright and headed for the back door, the dog following behind.

Gabe let her go. He stared at the stars and breathed in the night air and told himself to get a grip. Nothing was going to happen between him and Mary.

He'd been there when she needed a friend. And that's what they were: friends. He no more wanted to get anything romantic started with her than she did with him.

He sat in that plastic chair, staring up at the moon and the distant stars for a good half hour. By then, he had himself convinced that the weird moment of supposed jealousy hadn't been real. Just a bizarre emotional aberration brought on by their forced proximity over the past day and a half. Now that he'd dealt with it, now that he saw it for what it was, it wouldn't be happening again.

Eventually, he got up and went inside. The house was quiet. He slipped off his boots and left them at the door and took the few steps to the open door of the bedroom.

They were sleeping, both of them. Mary lay on her side, her arm curved protectively around her baby. He tiptoed into the room. Carefully, so as not to wake them, he lifted the folded afghan from the bottom of the bed and settled it over them. From the corner, he heard the thump of a tail on the floor. The dog gave a soft whine, and then with a sigh, put her head back on her paws and closed her eyes.

Gabe sneaked back out again, silently closing the door behind him, glad to see Mary conked out. She needed every minute of sleep she could get.

In the kitchen, he raided the refrigerator, helping himself to a mound of cold tuna casserole and a tall glass of milk. When he was through eating, he rinsed his dishes and put them in the dishwasher. About then, he heard a scratching sound from the bedroom. The dog wanted out. He opened the door a crack and she emerged. She went through the kitchen to the doggy door and he went on into the living room. At the alcove that enclosed the stairs, he hesitated. Mary had a spare room up there.

But no. Better to just stretch out on the couch, be nearby if she needed him. There was a blue blanket tossed across the armrest. He pulled it over him, grabbed the remote from the coffee table and switched on the TV very low, thinking it would keep him company until he finally fell asleep.

Turned out he didn't need it. He shut his eyes and he was over and out.

He didn't wake up till Ginny started crying a couple of hours later. He got up and went to the bedroom and found Mary in the rocking chair, nursing her. Mary rocked them gently back and forth.

She looked up and gave him the weariest smile. "Hey."

"How're you holding up?"

"I'm okay. Really. Go on back to sleep."

"I will. In a little while."

He took the straight chair in the corner and when the baby was through nursing, he got up and held out his arms.

Mary didn't argue. She gave him the diaper to put on his shoulder and then she gave him the baby.

"Get in bed," he told her, as he rocked Ginny slowly from side to side.

Mary pulled back the covers and got in, settling back on the pillow just as Ginny burped. And then filled her diaper.

Gabe chuckled. "Like clockwork, this girl."

Mary started to push the covers back. "I'll—"

"No way. Stay where you are. I can handle the diaper thing."

And he did. The smell and the mess were pretty awful. Other than that, nothing to it. He gave Ginny back to Mary when the job was done, and used her bathroom to wash his hands, figuring he'd go on back to his bed on the couch.

But Ginny kept fussing. Mary was getting up again to sit in the rocker with her when he came back into the bedroom.

"What's the problem?" he asked.

"I don't know. Maybe a little colic or something…"

"Give her to me."

"Oh, Gabe. You don't have to—"

"Give her to me and get back in bed."

Gabe hid a smile as she handed him the baby and got right back under the covers again. She was done in, without even the energy to argue with him.

"Sleep," he said, as Ginny wiggled on his shoulder and wailed into his ear.

Mary sighed and shut her eyes. Gabe left her alone, taking the baby out into the living room, where he walked the floor.

The walking did zero good. Ginny kept on fussing. Gabe rocked her from side to side and jiggled her gently. He patted her back and tried desperately to think of a lullaby to sing to her.

Since his mother had had him and his brothers and sisters one right after the other, he had been nine when Zoe, the youngest, was born. He didn't have any memories of how to calm a crying newborn. He was the damn fixer, and he couldn't make a baby stop wailing in his ear.

If it hadn't been well after midnight, he would have called his mom and asked her what to do. He might have called her anyway, even at that late hour. But his father would be there, in bed beside her. And as soon as he knew it was Gabe, he'd be grabbing the phone, demanding to know what the problem was.

Uh-uh. Gabe wasn't up for another Davis Bravo rant. He would handle this problem on his own. They didn't call him the fixer for nothing.

He began to experiment. He tried cradling her in his arms, face up. She cried louder. He put her on his other shoulder. Didn't help. But then he shifted her onto her stomach, laying her along his forearm, her legs to either side, her little head cradled in his hand.

Damned if that didn't seem to settle her down. She burped a couple of times. And then she yawned.

And went to sleep.

Gabe held her that way until his arm got tired. Then he put her to his shoulder again. She snuggled in and burped again, never even waking.

He dared to sit on the sofa, and then to carefully stretch out on his back, easing the baby down off his shoulder, so she slept on his chest. And then, gratefully, he closed his eyes.

When he woke the next time, it was five in the morning. And Ginny was awake and starting to fuss again. He carried her in to Mary, who was already getting out of bed to come and get her.

It went as before: Mary fed her, then Gabe took her, burped her and changed her.

"Go back to sleep," he told Mary and he took Ginny out into the living room with him again. Now that he knew the way to calm her, he laid her right on his arm. She sighed.

And slept.

Gabe stared down at the snoozing infant, thinking that he'd accomplished one or two pretty near-impossible feats in his four years as the family fixer. He'd charmed the most difficult clients and contacts into doing things everyone swore they would never do. He'd found a way to get his younger brothers out of some pretty rough situations, too. Once he'd even talked the Mexican authorities into releasing Jericho into his personal custody when they'd had him on a trumped-up drug trafficking charge and they'd made it more than clear they intended to keep him south of the border for a very long time.

Funny how figuring out a way to make Ginny stop crying in the middle of the night gave him every bit as much satisfaction as any of the major screw-ups he'd ever made right. As he lay down on the sofa again, and the baby snuggled on his chest, he almost laughed—except he was afraid he might wake her up.

"Losing it," he whispered softly, and kissed the top of Ginny's head. "I'm losing it, Ginny. I'm gone, gone, gone...."

And then he shut his eyes and went to sleep and when he woke up it was daylight and Mary was standing over him, wearing sweats and a T-shirt, the dog at her feet and Ginny in her arms.

He bolted to a sitting position. "What? She's hungry?"

"She was. I just fed her and changed her. If we're lucky, she'll go right back to sleep."

He heard a truck engine outside and turned to look over the back of the sofa as the old pickup rumbled past, headed around back.

"Just Garland," Mary said.

He rubbed his eyes. "I'll go out there and help him."

Mary felt better. Much better. It was partly that she was twenty-eight and healthy and quick to recover even from a tough job like having a baby. But it was also because Gabe had taken Ginny for most of the night, leaving her alone to get some much-needed sleep.

Another reason to be grateful to him. There were so many. It was getting kind of embarrassing how good he was to her. How much she owed him, her own private "fixer."

Should she be suspicious? Was that what was going on

here? He'd seen a way to get to her, to make her feel obligated? Was it all a way to work on her, to weaken her resolve until she finally said "yes" and sold him the Lazy H?

"Uh-uh." She said the denial right out loud.

She just didn't believe it. He knew she wouldn't sell. She'd told him enough times.

He was, quite simply, a better man than he even knew. He'd been good to her for no other reason than that she'd needed a helping hand. And now they were bound; they were true friends.

While Gabe was out with Garland, she put Ginny in her bassinet, fed Brownie and changed her water and then started making breakfast—enough for Garland, too. He came in with Gabe and she didn't have to twist his arm hardly at all to get him to share the meal with them.

Garland left at a little after seven.

"Take a nap," Gabe said. "I'll wake you when that helper you hired gets here."

Mary didn't argue. "If you insist on being so good to me, you just go ahead."

"Thanks," he said dryly. "I'll do that."

Her head hit the pillow and she was out like a light.

She slept until Ginny's fussing woke her. It was nine-fifteen. She picked up the crying baby and went out into the kitchen where Gabe sat at the table, answering e-mail on his laptop.

He glanced up. "I called my office. They know I'll be late. And I took a shower in the upstairs bathroom. I hope that's okay."

"Of course." Mary glanced toward the big window in the living room. "No sign of my home care specialist, huh?"

"Not yet."

Ginny kept fussing, so Mary took her back into the bedroom, sat in the rocker and fed her.

When the feeding and changing were done, it was nine forty-five. She picked up the phone and called the agency. They said the woman was on her way.

The phone rang just as she hung up. It was Ida.

Gabe came in from the kitchen as she was saying goodbye. He waited till she hung up. "Well?"

"My helper is on her way. And Ida called. Johanna's finally on a plane to St. Louis. Ida says she'll be back tomorrow. In the morning, if she can get a flight."

"Good. So call that agency back and tell them never mind."

Oh, she did want to do exactly that. Why would she want some stranger in her house when she could have Gabe? "Gabe. Really. No."

"It's only one more day," he argued. "I can manage it at work." He gestured toward the kitchen and the open laptop on the table in there. "I'm handling things well enough from here."

But she only shook her head again. "It's just not right."

At ten after ten, a dusty compact car finally pulled to a stop in front of the house. A girl got out. Slim, with long blond hair and a prairie dress—puffy sleeves, full skirt to mid-calf. Flat shoes. Mary watched her approach the front door with a sinking feeling. The girl couldn't be more than eighteen at the most. She looked younger. Barely more than a child.

"Hi," the girl said brightly when Mary opened the door. She had a wide, pretty smile and a face scrubbed clean of makeup. "I'm Whitney. Whitney Dale. And I'm so sorry. I know I'm late. I'm, well, I'm just really bad at directions." The smile faded. "I got lost." All at once, she looked like she might burst into tears. "I got all the way to Wulf City and then I had to ask at a gas station and then I didn't get those directions right. I ended up in New Braunfels. And then Gruene. It was awful, just awful…"

"It's okay. You're here now."

"Oh!" Her hand flew to her mouth. "I forgot the contract. I better…" She made a fluttery gesture back over her shoulder. "You know. In the car…"

"Go ahead."

"Okay. Great. Be right back." Whitney whirled and raced back down the steps.

Mary stood, staring after her, trying to tell herself that it would work out, that just because she *seemed* ditzy and way too young didn't mean she wasn't perfectly capable.

From her bed in the corner, Brownie let out a whine. Mary sent her a glance. She whined again, brown eyes soulful. Mary couldn't help thinking that even the dog seemed to have her doubts about this supposed home care specialist.

But then the girl came inside and sat on the couch, her dress fanning out around her like the petals of some country flower. She started talking. "Whew. I just want you to know, I'm new at this. And I'm not very good with babies. And I really hope you don't want me to cook. I'm a terrible cook. But I can clean—pretty well. And I'm real good company. The lady at the agency said you were pretty desperate." She smiled, looking perfectly angelic. "So I guess a beginner will be okay with you."

"Whitney." Gabe stood in the archway between the kitchen and the living room. "It *is* Whitney, right?"

She glanced his way and smiled even brighter. "Yes. Whitney. Right."

"I'm Gabe. Will you excuse us for just a minute?"

"Well, sure. Of course."

"Mary." He jerked his head in the direction of the back patio.

"Just a minute, then," she said to Whitney, and followed him out.

He shut the back door *and* the storm door, taking care that they both latched before he turned to her. "Tell her you won't need her after all. If you're uncomfortable with doing it, *I'll* tell her."

He was right, of course. But his being right wasn't the point. "It's not your decision, Gabe."

"You *were* going to send her away, weren't you?"

"Gabe—"

"You were only going to wait until I left so I wouldn't know and feel that I had to stay." It really wasn't fair. The man was always a couple of steps ahead of her. He came closer. So gently, he cradled her face between his hands. His palms were warm against her cheeks and he smelled of some light, tempting aftershave. "Well, I *do* know," he said. "So you don't need to wait until I'm gone."

She wrapped her fingers around his wrists. At her slight tug, his hands dropped away. And something scary happened within her—a sadness, a longing. She wished that he would touch her again, deliberately, the way he'd just done. Tenderly. The way a man will touch a wife.

Or a lover…

Of course, he wouldn't. They didn't have that kind of friendship. And she wasn't up for that sort of thing, anyway.

She stepped back. "I guess it's pointless to put it off."

"And end up signing all those papers she's got and committing yourself to paying her, wasting poor Ida's money?"

"Sheesh. Rub it in a little, why don't you?"

"So you agree, she has to go. Do you want me to tell her?"

"No. I'll take care of it."

He ushered her in ahead of him. She marched straight to where Whitney, round-eyed, sat on the sofa with her hands folded in her lap.

Mary got right down to it. She knew if she didn't, Gabe would do it for her. "Whitney, thank you so much for coming. But as it turns out, my mother-in-law will be here tomorrow to help me, so I won't be needing you after all."

An expression of purest relief crossed Whitney's pretty face. She jumped up. "You're sure?"

Mary nodded.

Whitney grabbed the papers she'd set on the coffee table and practically ran for the door. She hovered with her hand on the knob, her wide skirt swaying. "The truth is, I don't know if I'm cut out to be a home care specialist after all," she confessed in a guilty rush.

"I certainly understand," said Mary.

Whitney pulled open the door and got out of there, racing down the front steps and out to her car, as though scared to death that Mary might change her mind and call her back.

As the girl drove away, Gabe said, "I'll call the office."

She turned to him. "No. I can't let you—"

He didn't let her get going. "Just don't, all right? It's one more day—a half a day, really. It's not a big deal. Don't make it into one."

But it is *a big deal,* her heart cried. *It's a very big deal.*

Two days ago, he'd been a stranger. He came from a world she didn't even understand. She was starting to feel…things she shouldn't, about him. She wanted to lean on him.

No. Scratch that. She'd *already* been leaning on him.

The problem was, she wanted to go on leaning on him. Indefinitely.

And that just wasn't going to happen. They weren't from the same world. Soon enough, he'd go back to Bravo-Corp and his high-powered lifestyle—his *bachelor* lifestyle. And she would still be right here, on the land she loved. As she still loved Rowdy, even though he was gone. Here, with her good friends around her, with Ida to count on and her beautiful baby in her arms.

Gabe repeated, "One more damn day." He sounded so determined. And a little angry.

And maybe kind of hurt.

And a calmness suffused her. He was right, as usual. One day, and that was all. Tomorrow, Ida would be here, ready and more than able to give Mary the helping hand she needed.

Gabe would be able to leave her with a clear conscience, knowing she would be well cared for. Their time together would come to its own natural end. She didn't have to hurt him by sending him away when they both knew she still needed him.

She closed the distance between them. "Yes," she stared up into those gorgeous blue eyes, even allowed herself to reach up and frame his face with her hands, as he had done to her out on the back patio. His cheeks were smooth and fresh-shaved against her palms. "You're right, of course. As you always are."

"Uh. I am?" He stared down at her, thoroughly bewildered by her change of heart.

She nodded. "Yes. Absolutely. I'm being foolish, to push you away when you keep telling me you're willing to stay. I would be so grateful if you would stay until tomorrow when Ida gets here."

He looked kind of stunned. "You would?"

She let him go, stepping back. It wouldn't do to let the touch linger too long. "I would. You're wonderful to me and I'm so grateful. Thank you."

He cleared his throat. "Well. Good. It's settled, then."

"Yes. It's settled. Call your office."

Chapter Eight

Gabe had no idea what had changed Mary's mind. He just knew she'd done the right thing, finally, and let him stay while she needed him.

The day went by very much like the day before. He worked at the kitchen table. Mary cared for the baby. In the afternoon, Gabe took Ginny and told Mary to go have a nap. She didn't argue. She slept for two hours.

That evening, Donna Lynn dropped by again, with a cooked ham and a big plastic container of potato salad. Ida had called her, too, and told her that she would be back the next day.

While Donna Lynn was there, a couple of other friends from town stopped in. And Garland came early. They ended up sharing a meal with the food everyone had brought that day and the day before. It was fun, Gabe thought. Kind of a family feeling. Reminded him of times at Bravo Ridge, when they'd all sit around the big oak table in the kitchen, laughing and joking together.

Those times with his family didn't happen enough lately. They were all grown up now, and busy with their own lives. Sometimes Luke, the family's one born rancher, who lived at Bravo Ridge full time, complained that they all didn't get home often enough.

That night, like the night before, he and Mary sat out on the back patio, her dog, Brownie, stretched out between them. The sky was overcast and the air heavy and wet with the promise of rain. They watched lightning fork and heard low rumbles of thunder.

He told her about Ash. "He's the oldest. CEO of Bravo-Corp. He was engaged to marry Lianna Mercer."

Mary laughed, low and sweetly. And then she put on a snooty voice. "You mean Lianna Mercer of the San Antonio Mercers?"

He sent her a puzzled glance. "How'd you guess?"

"Something in the way you said her name. I could hear money and power and influence—and you also said your brother *was* engaged to marry her. Past tense. So it didn't work out?"

"Well, his plane crashed in the Sierras and he fell in love with the woman who rescued him. They were married in a little church in her hometown a month ago."

"Do they live here, in Texas?"

"They do. She's great. Tessa's her name. Big-hearted, you know? We're all half in love with her. And Ash is so happy."

She slanted him a look. "You sound surprised at that."

"You'd have to know Ash. Happy is not a word anyone would have used to describe him before. He was…driven. Ambitious. A lot like dear old Dad. But Tessa's kind of mellowed him. She's terrific." He dared to suggest, "You'd like her, I'll bet."

For that, he only got a smile. She asked, "So your brother broke Lianna Mercer's heart, is that what you're telling me?"

"Apparently not. Word is, Lianna broke up with *him*."

"Then it worked out fine for everyone."

"Yeah." The first raindrops spattered the dry ground beyond the patio cover and pinged on the metal overhead. Lighting flashed again, so bright, closer than any of the strikes before, followed by a grumble of thunder that built to a roar.

Brownie got up with a nervous whine and disappeared around the side of the house, probably headed for the dog entrance in the side door. From the bedroom, Ginny started crying.

Mary went in. Gabe lingered for a few minutes to listen to the hard patter of the rain overhead, thinking as he had the night before that with a little loving care the Lazy H would be a great place.

Again that night they took turns with the baby. At three in the morning, Gabe lay on the sofa with Ginny on his chest, feeling her warmth against his heart, thinking that he was doing a fine job here.

Ida Mae Hofstetter had better do as well. She'd better take damn good care of this baby. And of Mary, too.

Gabe smiled as the baby gave a huge yawn, smacked her little lips and sighed in her sleep. How could a man fall in love with a baby?

He had no idea. But whenever he held Ginny, his heart seemed to expand in his chest. Sure felt like love to him.

Outside, the rain had stopped, though the ozone smell of it still hung in the air. The house was quiet except for

Ginny's soft breathing. He closed his eyes and drifted just on the near side of sleep, feeling so peaceful inside himself, feeling happy in a way he'd never known before.

Yeah, he knew he was getting way too involved here. He knew it was bound to end in a few short hours. But he pushed that knowledge from his mind. He fell asleep with a smile on his face.

In the morning, he got up and helped Garland with the livestock. Then they all three had breakfast together. Gabe enjoyed the meal, the easy conversation, the fond way Mary treated Garland and the old man's gruff humor that couldn't mask his affection for Rowdy Hofstetter's widow.

When Garland left, Mary went in to take care of Ginny, who'd started fussing a little. Gabe straightened up the kitchen. Once the table was cleared and the dishes were in the dishwasher, he got out his laptop and pretended to work.

But he wasn't working. He was waiting.

For Mary's mother-in-law to get there. For the fast-approaching moment when he would be on his way.

The phone rang at a little after nine. Mary took it in the bedroom. He knew it was Ida. He heard the eagerness in Mary's voice, heard her say, "I can't wait to see you." His own phone vibrated more than once. He ignored it. He could deal with it later. No big rush.

He'd have the rest of his life to answer the damn phone.

At nine-thirty, he shut down his laptop and put it in the briefcase. He gathered the few belongings he had lying around and stuffed them back in the small suitcase he'd brought from his place Monday night. He put everything by the front door. Ready to go.

And then he went into Mary's room. He found her

sitting in the rocker, nursing Ginny. She looked up from the baby and gave him a smile.

And he couldn't stop himself. He went to her.

She gazed up at him as he approached, a thousand questions in those soft brown eyes. But all she said was his name on a rising inflection. "Gabe?"

He gave no answer. Except to bend down and press his lips to hers.

She gasped, a sweet, sharp intake of breath against his mouth. And then, for a brief, beautiful second or two, she opened to him. He tasted her, so sweet, so good…

And then, with a small, confused sound in her throat, she rocked back. He lost the warm taste of her.

She gazed up at him, stricken. "Oh, Gabe," she whispered. "I'm so sorry. I'm just…" She ran out of words.

He demanded roughly, "Just what?"

And she said it, she left no doubt. "I'm not ready for anything like this."

Chapter Nine

A few short minutes after Mary crushed all his wild, impossible hopes, Ida Hofstetter arrived. Tall and slim, with silver hair, a long, plain face and a square jaw, she had a capable look about her, strong and direct, both feet on the ground.

She brought two heavy suitcases in with her, one in each hand, the lean muscles in her long arms flexing beneath the short sleeves of her white shirt. And after she'd held her granddaughter and declared her the most beautiful baby in the world, she hugged Mary and told her how glad she was to be home at last.

"Oh, Ida." Mary hugged her back, hard. "Me, too."

Then Mary introduced them. "This is Gabe." She smiled widely at her mother-in-law, but when she looked at him, her gaze slid away.

Ida extended a hand and Gabe took it. She wrapped her other hand around their joined ones. Her hazel eyes were full of honest warmth. If he'd doubted that Mary's mother-in-law could remain unthreatened by finding another man in her dead son's house, taking care of his wife and baby, he doubted no more. "I've heard all you've done for Mary and the baby. I don't know what to say, except to thank you, with all of my heart."

"Always happy to help."

Ida beamed. "Well, you're a lifesaver and we can't thank you enough." She let go of his hand and held out her arms for Ginny again. "Oh, let me hold her. I am just aching to hold her."

Mary handed her over again. "I'll bet you want coffee."

Ida adjusted the baby's blanket, her eyes only for Ginny. "Now you're talkin'."

Mary laughed. "Well, come on in the kitchen, then."

Gabe saw the moment for what it was: time for him to go. He had to face reality now. He was no longer needed here.

And Mary's words of a few minutes before wouldn't stop echoing in his head. *I'm not ready for this.* She'd said it softly, not wanting to hurt him, but that didn't make her meaning any less clear.

He spoke up before they could wander into the kitchen, "Great to meet you, Ida." He turned to Mary. "Time I got out of here. There's more than one meeting I ought to be at today."

Ida did look up from the baby then. "Sure you can't stay for a last cup of coffee?"

"I'd love to. But I need to get going." He wanted to ask to hold Ginny one more time—but no. Holding that baby would only make leaving all the harder.

Better to cut it clean.

The damn ugly brown dog padded over and whined up

at him, as if she knew he was out of there. He knelt long enough to give her a scratch behind the ear.

"I'll walk you out," said Mary.

"Suit yourself. 'Bye, Ida. Great to meet you."

"You come back, now. Door's always open."

"Thanks." He reached for his stuff.

Mary followed him outside, where the scent of last night's rain still hung in the air and the big, blue sky was dotted with dark-bellied clouds. He went around to the driver's side, yanked open the door and tossed his stuff across the passenger seat.

Mary was right there. She stopped with the door between them and cleared her throat. "I, um, don't know what I would have done if you hadn't showed up here Monday morning, Gabe...." She did meet his eyes then. But in her gaze, he saw wariness. She didn't reach out, didn't edge around the door to get a little closer to him. The barrier it made seemed to suit her just fine.

"Glad I could help. You take care. And give Ginny a kiss for me."

The wind toyed with her hair, blowing the shiny brown strands across her cheeks. He gripped the top of the door, hard, to keep himself from reaching out and guiding those strands out of her eyes.

She smoothed them back. "I will. Goodbye, Gabe."

Goodbye. Not *see you later* or *see you soon.* Uh-uh. *Goodbye.* Didn't get much clearer than that. Whatever it was between them, it was over without ever really getting started.

He stepped up behind the wheel. "'Bye, Mary." He pulled the door shut and revved the engine, giving her one last wave as he put it in gear.

She waved back. He couldn't resist glancing in the

rearview mirror as he left her behind. She stood there waving, the wind blowing her shining hair, ruffling the hem of the loose shirt she wore, until he turned the corner to go around the house and she disappeared from view.

She was gone when he headed back down the driveway to the road. He told himself it was for the best. Mary was still in love with her dead husband.

And Gabe wasn't the settling-down kind anyway. Better to let it go. Too damn bad about that tight feeling in his chest, the strange ache that made him wonder if he'd just lost everything that mattered in the world.

As if a man could lose a thing he'd never had in the first place.

Gabe went to his big, modern house in Alamo Heights, not far from the house where Ash lived with his new bride. The place seemed empty as a politician's promise. He thought with the weirdest stab of longing of Mary's ugly mutt, Brownie.

Maybe he ought to get himself a dog or something.

He no sooner considered the idea than he rejected it. Between his killer work hours and his social life, a dog would die of loneliness waiting for him to come home.

He changed into business clothes and went down to his four-car garage. He took the Jag to the BravoCorp building.

Georgia, who was every bit as gorgeous as she was capable, granted him her cute dimpled smile when he got off the elevator at his floor. "You're here. Great."

"Give me five minutes. We'll go over everything."

"Got a month?"

"No, but I have faith in you. Work up a short version, just the main points."

While Georgia was bringing him up to speed, he let the front desk take his calls. But when his father buzzed him, he picked up.

"It's about time you got here," Davis growled.

"You're slipping, Dad," Gabe teased, trying to establish a lighter tone. "Took you a full half hour to find out I was in the building."

Davis had no intention of lightening up. "Don't give me attitude. We need to talk. My office. Ten minutes."

"I'll be there." He hung up and nodded at Georgia. "Continue."

His assistant never failed to amaze him. In another seven minutes, she had him fully caught up on everything he'd missed. She returned to her desk to start working through the list of new tasks he'd given her. And he went up one floor to his father's office, which had windows on three sides and great views of the Riverwalk and the Alamo.

Davis was waiting in that giant oxblood-leather swivel chair of his, behind his heavily carved mahogany desk, San Antonio spread out behind him. He looked like the king of Texas. Which he more or less considered himself. He wore Armani—because he could. And at fifty-eight, he was still a handsome man, with erect posture, broad, straight shoulders and a belly that didn't hang over his belt.

Ash, not only the oldest of Gabe's brothers, but also CEO of BravoCorp, was there, too. Davis didn't rise from his throne-like chair when Gabe entered, but Ash got up.

"Gabe." His big brother came toward him, wearing a smile. Since he'd lost his memory in California and found it again—along with his new wife, Tessa—Ash smiled a lot. He even held out his arms for a hug.

Gabe hesitated. Even lately, since he'd married Tessa,

Ash wasn't *that* affectionate. But as soon as he got his arms around Gabe, his real intention became clear.

He whispered, "Watch your ass. He's on the warpath."

Gabe already knew that. One look at Davis's face had made the coming storm perfectly clear. Still, he clapped his brother on the back to let him know he appreciated the warning.

"Have a seat." Davis made the offer into a command. "Both of you." They took the leather armchairs opposite the desk. Davis wasted no time getting to the point. "I've got a meeting set up. Ten o'clock tomorrow morning, with everyone involved in the Bravo River project." Davis's ice-green gaze bored into Gabe. "We postponed the meeting Tuesday since you couldn't make it to give your report. Now we're on for tomorrow. I just wanted to make sure about you beforehand."

Gabe sat back in the chair, faking an ease he didn't feel. "I'll be there."

"All right, then. And you'll give your report."

"Sure."

"What's the downstroke?"

"Meaning?"

"Give your brother and me a preview."

"What do you need, Dad?" As if he didn't already know. As if Davis didn't *know* he knew. But it would only put Gabe in a weakened position to name the main issue before his father did.

Davis quit dangling the carrot and said it, flat out. "I need you to tell me Mary Hofstetter's on board. Now, before the meeting. Better still, I want to see her signature on the relevant pages of that more than generous offer we sent you to make to her. You've had since Monday to work that woman around to the right point of view. For you, that's more than enough time and we both know it is."

Gabe went ahead and laid it on him. "I can't tell you she's on board. She's not on board. She's never getting on board. She isn't going to sell. And while I was out of the office, I did some research online. I've found two other properties that might work for the project. I think we ought to—"

Davis put up a hand. "I didn't ask you to find other properties. I sent you out to do your job, which is to fix this situation."

"There is no fixing it. We need to move on."

"I want that land."

"You won't get it."

"I'll do what I have to do."

Gabe had been kind of worried it might come to this. To threats and dirty dealing. Shades of Grandpa James. While Davis was usually above such tactics, now and then, he went too far.

Ash spoke up. "Dad."

Davis turned his lowering gaze on his older son. "You got a solution? Great."

"Only this. If the woman's firm on not selling, why not check into the other possibilities?"

"Because that land is perfect for the project. We've already eliminated the other possibilities. You both know that."

"Times are tough," Gabe said. "What wasn't available six months ago is going for a damn song today."

"Gabe's right," said Ash. "Let's have a look at what he's found. We can—"

Davis's big fist hit the desktop. And when he spoke, it was much too softly. "Gabe. Go back to the widow again today. Don't leave until she's agreed to sell."

Ash started to speak.

Gabe stopped him with a hand on his arm. "I'll say it once more. Mary Hofstetter is not selling the Lazy H. We need to find somewhere else to build Bravo River."

A silence. A bad one. Then Davis folded his hands on his desk blotter and leaned toward his second son. "What the hell is going on with you, Gabe?"

"Not a thing."

"You vanished for three days with hardly more than a word. That's not like you. Something is up. You been sleepin' in the widow's bed, is that it? You got a soft spot for a Hill Country nobody when you can have any damn woman in the whole state of Texas?"

Gabe gripped the chair arms to keep from leaping up and punching the old man's lights out for calling Mary a nobody. But he answered honestly. "No. I'm not sleeping with Mary. She turned me down."

He watched with satisfaction as his father gaped. "She what?" Davis demanded as Ash choked on a laugh.

Gabe seized the moment. "You heard what I said. Mary turned me down. But that's not the issue. The thing is, I do have a soft spot for her. I'm real fond of her and I don't want her bothered. I don't want you going too far with this, making life difficult for a good woman who only asks that you leave her alone. So I'm going to need your promise that BravoCorp will look elsewhere for the Bravo River property."

Davis seethed. "No way will you get my word on that. I want that land. If you want off this project, fine. You're off. I'll find someone else to convince the widow to sell."

It was a step, Gabe thought. If his father was willing to let him off the hook on this, maybe the light was beginning to dawn.

He tried one more time to get Davis to see reason. "You've sent four men already, including me. How many ways can the woman say no? She's not going to sell. The sooner you accept that, the sooner you can find someone who will."

But Davis held firm. "Enough. I'm not accepting any such thing."

Ash stopped by Gabe's desk later. "Give me what you've got on those other properties you found. I'll put a couple of people on it, have them go out and have a look at what's out there. And talk price. If Dad sees it on paper, if it's there in black and white that he can get exactly what he wants from someone who's actually looking to sell…he'll snap out of it."

"I hope you're right." Gabe had Georgia give him the files.

The next morning, Gabe's mother was waiting for him when he got to the office, looking great as always in a soft red sweater and snug gray slacks, her brown hair cut short and sleek, which brought out those gorgeous blue eyes of hers.

She jumped up and kissed his cheek. "Can you spare me five minutes?"

He took her by the shoulders and gazed at her fondly. *You love your mom,* Mary had said. *That's good. A man should love his mom….*

The memory hurt. Because he wished he was back there, sitting beside her in the plastic chair under that tin awning. Just talking. Just being there, with her.

"Gabe?" His mom looked worried. She touched his face. "What is it?"

"Not a thing." He gave her his most charming smile. "This way." He led her into his office. "Coffee?"

"No, thanks." She took a chair in the conversation area near the door. "I'm so glad to see you're all right. We did get worried when we didn't hear from you at the first of the week."

"I'm good, Mom. Fine. Sorry to be out of touch."

She set her purse on the side table next to her. "All right, then. Just checking." She sent him a look. The one that said she really wanted to push for more information, but she wouldn't.

"So what can I do for you?" he asked.

"Well." She sat back, crossed her ankles and delicately turned her knees to the side. He knew then. Something in the movement, both elaborate and too casual, tipped him off. She asked, "Do you remember Tippy Onstott? We went to UT together, back before the dawn of time."

"Vaguely. Tippy has a couple of daughters, right?"

She slanted him a look. "That's right. Arabella and Courtney. Arabella married Chance Doubray just last year."

"So then, it's about Courtney."

His mother laughed. "Gabe. Don't look so grim. You're usually only too happy to meet my friends' daughters. And Courtney is lovely, truly."

"I'm sure she is."

Aleta thought it was time Gabe found a good woman and settled down, and she was always trying to help him with that. Usually, Gabe was happy to take out the "suitable" women she chose for him. Though nothing ever came of her matchmaking, his mother kept trying. And Gabe enjoyed women. Plural. He knew how to treat a lady, so it always worked out fine.

But now the thought of meeting Courtney Onstott only made him feel tired.

Aleta sat straighter. "Something's wrong. Your father told me that someone you really like turned you down."

"Mom. Come on. 'Someone I really like?' That's not what he said."

"It was…what he meant."

Gabe let that pass. "He shouldn't have said anything."

"We don't keep secrets, your father and I. It's one of the reasons we've lasted so long."

"Have you told Courtney or her mother that you want to introduce us?"

Aleta looked honestly hurt. "I would never do that without your okay."

"Good, then. I'm sure Courtney's beautiful and smart and fun to be with…."

"But you don't want to go out with her."

"Not this time, Mom. Thanks."

"At the risk of sticking my nose in where it's not welcome, sometimes it helps, in a situation like this, to go out with someone else, to have a little fun, just for fun's sake."

If he wanted fun for fun's sake he could hook up with Carly again. But he wouldn't.

And he wouldn't be going out with the lovely and suitable Courtney Onstott, either.

Damn. This was bad. He really should snap out of it.

And he would, he kept telling himself. He would forget Mary. He just needed a little time.

On Monday, a week after Ginny was born, Ida moved back to her house in town. That afternoon, a woman in high heels, a pencil skirt and a great-looking jacket rang Mary's doorbell.

Her name was Emily Gray and she was from Bravo-Corp. She had a beautiful, friendly smile and she couldn't wait to present Mary with another of those offers that Mary wasn't supposed to be able to refuse. Mary turned her down politely.

"Emily," she said. "I'm so sorry you had drive all the way out here. I've said 'no' to selling my place four times before you. I'm not going to change my mind."

"I know you're hesitant, Mary. That's what I'm here for. To help you get past your fears."

"Honestly, I'm not fearful. I just don't want to sell."

"Mary—"

"Goodbye, Emily. Sorry you had to waste your time." Mary shut the door.

After a moment, she heard the sharp tap-tapping of Emily's high heels as she turned and went back down the steps. A minute later, Emily's car started up. There was the crunch of tires on gravel as she pulled away.

Mary listened to the car drive off, the sound of it backing and turning, and then fading into the distance. She was crying, out of nowhere, big old tears just running down her face.

She wished that Emily had been Gabe. She wished it with all her heart.

Oh, she missed him so, even though she kept telling herself that missing him was stupid and pointless and she needed to get over it. She'd sent him away. She'd told him no.

And now she wanted him back?

She was starting to remind herself of the kind of woman she couldn't stand. A woman who told a man to get lost— and then cried because he left.

She kept telling herself to snap out of it, but she couldn't stop thinking about him. She, well, she longed for him. She did. She wished she could turn back time to that kiss they'd shared. If she had another chance, she would ask him to do that again—not push him away.

But she'd gotten scared, that was all.

And she was still scared.

The minute Gabe's lips met hers…it had been like a door opening. Into a kind of yearning she'd never felt before. The love she'd felt for Rowdy was a sweet love, and gentle. Safe.

This new feeling she had for Gabe?

Like a fire, burning. Not safe in the least.

Oh, please. She was a single mom on a limited income with a newborn to care for. She needed to keep her mind on her baby and making a living. She had no time for romance.

Mary swiped the pointless tears from her cheeks and told herself for the hundredth time to get over this silliness. Gabe Bravo was not the man for her.

From the bedroom, Ginny started fussing. Mary put her hopeless yearning away and went to feed her daughter.

Ginny's first checkup, the next day, went great. Dr. Breitmann said she'd gained two ounces, even though Mary's milk had only come down the Friday before.

Mary was doing well, too, healing quickly, feeling more her old self every day. She went back to her desk on Wednesday for three full hours. And she worked on Thursday, too. She turned in the canning article on Friday and got going on the next couple of projects she had in the works. She had everything to be happy about and nothing to mope over.

But still, she did mope. She had that burning desire for a certain smooth, rich lawyer. It didn't go away. She kept telling herself that time was what she needed. In a month or two, she'd be saying, "Gabe, who?"

The following Monday, a week after her previous visit, Emily Gray came to see Mary again, at seven in the evening. She wasn't smiling this time.

"Before you shut that door on me, Mary," she said, her voice coated in ice, "I just want you to consider how foolish you're being. I hate to have to say this, but things could get unpleasant if you don't see reason."

Mary blinked. "Is that a threat?"

"Of course not. Let me in and we'll work this out."

Mary wanted to spit in Emily's perfectly made-up face. But she didn't. She held it together. "I'm sorry. Nothing you can say to me is going to make a difference. Goodbye."

"Mary, wait—"

But Mary had already shut the door. She twisted the lock for good measure as Emily rang the doorbell again and called her name.

"Mary. Mary, please…"

Mary did nothing. She waited until she heard high heels tap-tap-tapping back across the porch. Then she sagged against the door. And started crying just like she had the last time.

Ida, who'd come by to help with dinner and spend some time with the baby, emerged from the bedroom holding Ginny before Mary could pull herself together.

"My Lord," said Ida. "What in the world…?"

Mary told herself to suck it up and stop blubbering. Now. But she only cried harder, in great, gulping sobs. "Ida. Oh, Ida…"

"Wait right there," said her mother-in-law. "Do not move. I'm just going to put Ginny in her bassinet…."

She was back in under a minute, reaching for Mary, pulling her into her capable arms, clucking her tongue, saying, "There now, you cry, now. It's all right. It's okay."

Mary clung to her, whimpering like some spoiled, self-indulgent baby. "Oh, I just hate myself. This is so…dumb…."

"Of course it's not dumb. It's not dumb in the least. You feel what you feel and sometimes you just need to cry it out. Now, you come on. Come over here to the sofa…" She guided Mary down and handed her a couple of tissues.

Mary blew her nose and wiped her eyes and then just sat there, gulping back more sobs, wishing the floor would open up and swallow her whole. "I'm such a fool…."

"You are no fool. You are one of the *least* foolish people I know." Ida sat down next to her and put an arm around her shoulders. "Come on," she coaxed, reaching over to smooth Mary's hair out of her eyes. "Talk about it. Talking always helps."

"Oh, Ida. I just…" How to say it? "I don't know what to tell you. I don't know how to even begin."

Ida prompted, "Who was that at the door?"

"Her name's Emily. Emily Gray. BravoCorp sent her."

"Another offer on the ranch? But haven't you told them you're not going to sell?"

"I have, yes. Over and over. She came last week and I told her no. And this time, well, she kind of threatened me. She said how if I didn't see reason, things could get unpleasant. And it scared me a little."

"Well, I should think so."

"And I wished she was Gabe, but I know that's so stupid. Because I sent him away and now all I can think about is how he's not here…." She dissolved into sobs again.

Ida passed her more Kleenex and waited. When Mary

had pulled it together somewhat, she asked, "Does Gabe know about how his company is threatening you?"

"It wasn't a *big* threat...." Mary's voice trailed off. Ida only looked at her with an expression of limitless patience. "Oh," Mary cried. "I don't know. How would I know? I haven't talked to him since the day you got home. I...I told him I wasn't ready, you know, to get anything started with him."

"But it turns out you're more ready than you thought?"

"Ida. Come on. You, of all people, know how I loved my husband. I loved him so much."

"Of course you did. And you made Rowdy happy— happier than he ever knew he could be. He'd always been the quiet type, kind of shy. But you opened him up, Mary."

Mary dabbed more tears away. "It was a good marriage."

"I know." Ida's eyes were full of gentle understanding. "But he's gone. And he would want you to be happy, to find love again."

"Oh, Ida..."

"You need to stop dithering." Ida grabbed the phone from the coffee table. She took Mary's hand and slapped the phone into it. "Call Gabe Bravo. Do it now."

"Oh, no. I couldn't."

"Of course you can."

"Oh, Ida. I Googled him."

Ida didn't know from Google. "You what?"

"I looked him up on the Internet. And I found out he's just about the most eligible bachelor in the south half of Texas, with a different woman on his arm every night— gorgeous, glamorous women, Ida. He's known as the Bravo Bachelor. They actually called him that in *San Antonio Monthly*. And there's constant speculation over which beautiful, wealthy socialite will win his ring on her finger...."

"Mary, that's neither here nor there."

"What? Of course, it's—"

"Call him. Talk to him. Ask him to meet you for coffee or something. And when you see him, you can ask him if he knows that his company has threatened you. See if he can do something to get them off your back."

"But I just told you. I can't do it. I can't call him. I sent him away. He doesn't want to hear from me."

"Okay," said Ida. "*Now* you're acting like a fool."

Mary scowled at her mother-in-law. "Sometimes I hate it that you're always right."

Chapter Ten

Gabe almost didn't check his BlackBerry when it vibrated.

He was in the office late, going over a couple of prospective projects that Ash had passed to him for review and input, marking the spots where they would need to check further into the various legal ramifications before they decided whether or not to move forward. It was the kind of boring detail work that required strict concentration, and that was good. It helped him keep his mind off hopeless thoughts of Mary. So when his Black-Berry started buzzing, he should have left it to check later.

But something made him reach for it and glance at the display. He didn't recognize the number and that intrigued him.

He answered, "Gabe Bravo."

"Hi. It's Mary."

Mary. She said her name and it hit him like a kick in the gut. All he could do was say it back to her. "Mary…" Somehow he managed to add a rough, "Hi." And then terror struck. "My God. Ginny. Is she—?"

"Gabe. She's fine. Truly. She's just fine."

His racing heart slowed. But only a little. "Good." He took a careful breath. "Good."

"It's not about Ginny, don't worry. And I didn't mean to scare you, I just…Gabe, I wonder, could I come to your office, or meet you for coffee, maybe tomorrow sometime?"

His office or a coffee shop. Why? "What's this about?"

"It's kind of difficult. I'd rather talk face-to-face."

"I'll be right over."

He heard her small gasp and almost smiled. She started objecting. "No, really. It's not right that you should have to—"

"Half an hour." He hung up before she could tell him again not to come.

His business clothes weren't going to work. If he'd wanted a business meeting with her, he would have agreed to see her at BravoCorp.

He had a pair of jeans and a knit shirt in the dressing alcove off of the private bath in his office, so he went ahead and changed into them before he left. Then he stood at the mirror over the sink and rubbed his cheeks: serious stubble. He shaved, fast. By some miracle, he managed not to nick himself. He slapped on a little aftershave and combed his hair, feeling like a damned idiot—that it mattered so much, to look good for Mary. That he couldn't help hoping she'd maybe changed her mind, hoping that she'd re-thought the situation and decided she was ready to get something going with him, after all. Or at least, to *talk* about getting something going.

Unbelievable. All Mary had to do was call and he was falling all over himself like some teenager with his first big crush.

Once on the highway, he drove too fast. But the traffic gods smiled on him and he didn't get stopped. Twenty-nine minutes after hanging up the phone, he turned into Mary's driveway.

He pulled to a stop in front of the house and killed the engine. The sun had set a while before and full dark was maybe half an hour away. Her porch light popped on as he got out of the car. She appeared, opening the front door, pushing wide the storm door, too, as he came up the steps. She looked so pretty and sweet in jeans and a tight pink T-shirt. The porch light picked up red and gold gleams in her shiny brown hair.

He went in, getting that faint, tempting hint of soap and lemons as he passed her at the door. Her dog was there, just past the threshold, whining in greeting. He bent to give her a pat on the head.

"Hi," Mary said as he straightened.

He wanted to grab her and kiss her. "Hi."

They stared at each other. It was awkward. Strange. His blood was pumping so fast through his veins it made his ears ring.

Finally, she cleared her throat. "Thank you. For coming."

"It's all right." It came out flat. Expressionless. He was known for his smooth ways with women. Where was his legendary charm when he needed it?

She closed the curtain across the front window against the growing darkness outside and gestured toward the sofa. "Have a seat."

He stayed where he was. "Ginny?"

"She's great. Sleeping. You want to see her?" At his nod, she led the way to the bedroom.

Careful to be quiet, he went to the bassinet. Ginny lay on her back, sound asleep, her tiny pink fists resting on either side of her head. He ached to hold her. Maybe he'd get lucky and she'd wake up before Mary finished telling him whatever she'd called him to say.

Mary left the door open a crack so she could hear if Ginny cried, and they went back to the living room.

"She's bigger." He sat on the sofa.

Mary nodded. "Babies do tend to grow."

"Right."

"You look…rested." She took the chair across from him.

"You, too. How's Ida?"

"Good. Great. She was here, earlier. But she…went on home."

"Ah." He'd had enough of this tortured small talk. He went for it. "So why did you call me?"

"I…" She swallowed, licked her lips. He imagined himself grabbing her, yanking her close, kissing her, hard, sucking her tongue into his mouth—and then he wondered if she read his desire on his face, because she pulled her tongue back in sharply and pressed her lips together.

"Just tell me." He made his voice gentle. "It can't be all that bad."

"Right," she said. "I will. I am. Um, last Monday, in the morning, I had a visit from…" She fell silent. They both heard the footsteps outside on the porch.

He frowned at her. "Who's that?"

"Not a clue." She was already up, answering the door before whoever it was could ring the bell—and possibly wake up Ginny. "Yes?" She pushed the storm door open a few inches.

A male voice mumbled something.

Mary smiled. "Of course. Hungry?"

The voice said, "Yeah. I am."

"Tell you what, meet you around back at the kitchen door. I've got some extra brisket. I can make you a sandwich…."

"That would be great."

"Five minutes—and don't knock, okay? My baby's sleeping."

The guy said something else and she nodded and shut the door. She turned to Gabe. "This'll only take a minute."

"Sure." For lack of anything better to do with himself, he followed her to the kitchen and watched her slap a bunch of meat on a slice of bread. She slathered it in barbecue sauce, added the other slice of bread and cut it in half. Then she slid it on a paper plate, took three cookies from a jar and put them on the plate, too. She worked fast, turning once to smile at him, but not saying anything, not telling him what the hell was going on.

When the food was ready, she switched on the back patio light and opened the door. Gabe lurked behind her to get a look at whoever was out there.

It was no one he knew. The guy looked like a drifter. He had hard times written all over him—from his worn-out rawhide boots to the dirty backpack slung over one shoulder.

Mary gave him the food. He thanked her. She shut the door, but Gabe could still see through the glass top of it.

He watched the man amble across the backyard. "He's going to the barn." He turned to Mary.

She shrugged. "Yeah. I said he could sleep there. He

needs a place. And when people need a place, I generally give them one—if they look okay to me, I mean."

Gabe couldn't believe it. "Mary. You're here alone. With a baby. And you let some stranger bed down in your barn?"

She folded her arms under her breasts. "I don't like your tone, Gabe."

He wanted to grab her and shake her. "It's not safe. That man could murder you in your bed." He didn't realize he'd amped up the volume until she hissed at him.

"Shh!" She tipped her head toward the bedroom where Ginny slept and then turned for the living room.

Gabe fell in behind her. When they got to the sofa, she made a motion for him to sit, but he stayed on his feet.

She didn't sit either. And then she spoke, carefully. "I do appreciate your concern. But it's my choice if I want to help people. It's not much, a bed in the barn and a sandwich. But it's something I can do. Times are tough for a lot of folks. Someone's got to reach out a hand now and then. I have good locks on my doors and windows. Nobody's going to hurt me or Ginny."

"You don't know that guy. You have no idea what he might—"

"Will you just let it go, please?"

Let it go? He wanted to shout at her. He wanted to argue with her until she saw the light. He wanted to march out to the barn and tell the guy out there that Mary had people looking out for her and he'd damn well better not try anything stupid.

But he knew it would be totally out of line to take the subject any further. It was Mary's house and Mary's barn.

She had a right to do what she wanted with what was hers—and to suffer the consequences, if it came to that.

"Your life, Mary," he said, wanting to break something, yet careful to keep his voice neutral.

"That's right. My life." She stood a few feet from him, and she kept her arms wrapped around herself. "Now, can we get back to the reason I asked you here?"

"Sure."

"I…" She looked away, sucked in a slow breath, and then finally met his eyes again. "A week ago today, Emily Gray came to see me."

So. Yet another offer. He knew Emily. She was smart and ambitious. "Did you let her in?"

The corner of her mouth lifted in an almost-smile. "I did not."

"Good for you. Don't let them get to you."

"I won't. I haven't. Or, I wouldn't…"

"You want me to try and get BravoCorp to leave you alone, is that it? My dad's a tough customer, but I'll see what I can do." He'd check with Ash first, see where he'd gotten on the other possible properties.

Mary pulled her shoulders back. "Really, I can take it. I mean, if BravoCorp wants to send one fast talker after another out here, I say bring 'em on. It's not that they won't stop coming. It's that Emily Gray came again this evening and she wasn't so friendly this time."

He understood then. "She threatened you?" Was he surprised? Hardly. He'd just hoped the old man wouldn't go this far, but he'd only been kidding himself. To get what he wanted, Davis Bravo would go as far as he had to go.

Mary raked spread fingers through her hair. "She told me that if I didn't 'see reason,' things could get 'unpleasant.'"

Gabe swore, low. Here he was getting all over her case about some bum sleeping in her barn, when the real threat was his own damn company—and his father most of all. He cleared the short distance between them, wanting to reach for her, but thinking better of it just in time.

Instead, he put a reassuring hand on her shoulder. "I'll take care of it, Mary. One way or another, I'll make sure BravoCorp leaves you alone from now on."

"Oh, Gabe…" Her eyes were brimming.

And then *she* reached for him. Out of nowhere, she was in his arms. He could hardly believe it: Mary. In his arms.

At last.

He held her close, kissed her shining lemon-scented hair, rocked her gently, like a baby, from side to side and whispered, "It's okay. It'll be okay, I swear to you…" She held him so tight, her warm, soft body pressing all along his. Gabe knew he had to be dreaming.

But it was no dream. And it got better. She had her head buried tight against his shoulder. But then she looked up, her eyes bright as diamonds with the soft sheen of tears. "Oh, Gabe. When I sent you away…."

"Yeah?" He whispered the word around the tightness in his throat.

"It was only because I didn't know…how to handle it. How to deal with the way I feel about you. I got scared, Gabe. I've been…wishing, you know? Wishing that maybe you'd give me another chance."

He smoothed a hand down her hair, so silky and warm, and dared to press his palm to the side of her sweet face. Because he could. Because she wanted him, after all. Mary wanted another chance.

"Gabe." She said his name on a breathless sigh. "Is there maybe a chance that you'd want to try again? Is there maybe a—"

"Mary."

"What?"

"Yeah."

"There is?"

"Yeah. Kiss me, Mary."

"Oh, yes. Oh, Gabe…." She lifted her sweet mouth.

And he took it.

He meant to be gentle, to go easy, to take it slow. But the touch of her lips was like a match to tinder. With a hungry groan, he speared his tongue inside.

And she didn't deny him. Not this time. With a soft cry, she opened for him. He tasted her, deeply, a kiss that plundered, a kiss meant to claim her, a kiss to make up for the last week and a half of being without her.

Of longing for her, aching for her, and knowing at the same time that he had to give it up, to forget her. To move on.

All that was over now. She wanted him, after all. She wanted to try again.

They would be lovers. She would be his. It seemed impossible.

But no. It was real. True.

He took her face between his hands and lifted his mouth enough to whisper her name, "Mary. Mary, Mary…" And then he kissed her some more, long and hard and deep.

She didn't pull away. She kissed him back. Giving him her mouth to taste, even sliding her sweet tongue along his, entering his mouth as he had tasted hers, shyly, hesitantly, with a tender, yearning sigh.

He couldn't get enough of her, of the feel of her in his

arms. He ran his hand down her slim back, pressing hard into her, loving her softness, aroused out of all proportion by her full breasts pushing into his chest. He spread his hands and cupped her bottom, fingers digging in, pulling her up to him, so she could feel him, so she could know how much he needed her.

A low, hungry moan escaped her. He kissed her, harder, taking that moan into him, drinking the sound, drinking *her*.

He needed to touch her all over, every inch of her. He needed her naked.

He needed that now.

He slipped his hands up under the hem of that little pink shirt and felt the warm, smooth flesh of her back, of her rib cage. Amazing, to be touching her, to have his hands on her. He touched the strap of her bra and followed it back to the center and began working the hooks to release them.

But she caught his arms. And then she pulled away. "Gabe…" Lost in his need for her, he tried to capture her mouth again, but she wouldn't let him. "Gabe." She slid her hands up to capture his face. "Gabe, I can't."

He sucked in a slow breath, regaining shaky control of himself and repeated, not getting it, "You can't…?"

"No." She whispered the word, her sweet mouth trembling. "It's only been two weeks since I had Ginny. It's not safe for me yet."

"Not safe," he repeated after her, like some kind of idiot, still not really getting what she was telling him.

"Oh, Gabe." She looked up at him, her face flushed, her expression regretful.

And finally, he realized what she was trying to tell him. He shut his eyes. "God. I'm so sorry."

And she laughed, the sweetest, gentlest sound. "Don't be. Please. I wish it *was* safe. Oh, I really, really do…"

He pressed his forehead to hers. "You're not mad, that I got all over you?"

"Oh, Gabe. Why would I be mad about something as wonderful as that?"

He kissed her lips again—but softly this time. "Okay, if you're not mad, then tell me…"

She knew the question without his having to ask it. "How much longer?" At his nod, answered herself, "Usually, it's about six weeks."

"Four more weeks. I don't know if I can make it."

"Be strong," she teased.

"I will, considering I have no choice." He scooped her high in his arms. She let out an "Oh!" of surprise, and then she sighed, wrapped her arms around his neck and leaned her head against his chest. It was three steps to the sofa. He took them, turning to sit with her still in his arms so she ended up in his lap. She felt really good there. He nuzzled her hair, whispered in her ear, "Let me stay the night. I'll sleep right here, on the couch."

She read him so easily. "Stop worrying about that poor guy in the barn. He's not going to hurt me."

He kissed her cheek. "I've missed this couch since you sent me away. And besides, I'll be up and out of here good and early." He would meet with Davis first thing, make it crystal clear to the old man that Mary was under his protection now and all harassment was to cease. Now. "Mary…" He kissed her ear.

"Um?" She sighed and turned her head so their lips could meet.

He kissed her slow and deep, trying to keep a rein on it since there was only so far they could go—trying, but not completely succeeding. She moaned and moved against him. He felt himself hardening again.

It was sweet, hot torture. Mary drove him crazy. Just stark, raving out of his mind. Who knew that smart, no-nonsense Mary Hofstetter could drive a man wild with desire?

She pulled away enough to whisper, "We should stop."

"One more kiss."

"Oh, Gabe…" She gave in, offering that mouth of hers, opening to him so he could taste the wet sweetness within.

He was the one to end it that time, putting a finger under her chin, lifting his mouth away enough to whisper, "You taste so good. I don't want to stop. But you need to know I'm a man who keeps his word."

Brown eyes shone. "Oh, I do. I know it." With one last, quick press of her lips to his, she slid off his lap and stood. "You really ought to go."

The *ought to* was the giveaway. He knew then that she would let him stay. He spread his arms wide along the back of the couch and crossed one booted foot on the opposite knee. "That brisket sure looked good…."

Mary felt a glow all through her. Like the world was magic and the magic was centered smack dab in the center of her heart.

She made Gabe a sandwich and gave him a beer. Then she sat at the table with him and watched him eat, her chin on her hand, thinking how much she'd missed seeing him there, across from her, the past lonely days.

Was this love, then?

She hesitated to say so. Yet. It was like no other feeling

she'd ever known. She had loved Rowdy deeply, a love steady and strong.

But this? This was something altogether new. Sparkly like fireworks. Fizzy like champagne.

She'd done what her heart told her to do—with a little nudge from Ida. And now she was just going to go with it, follow the magic wherever it took her.

After Gabe ate, she popped a bowl of popcorn and they watched an old movie on one of the movie channels. Ginny woke up in the middle of it. Gabe went and got her.

It was the strangest thing. He carried the baby out into the living room and she lay in his big arms, kind of staring up at him, perfect pink hands waving, making the sweetest little cooing sounds—as if she knew him, remembered him. As if she was happy to see him again. Mary got all dewy-eyed, just watching that.

In a minute or two, Ginny remembered she was hungry. She started fussing and Gabe handed her over. Mary fed her, sitting right there on the couch next to Gabe, feeling completely comfortable about nursing in front of him.

It was still just so…relaxed and natural between them. As if they'd picked up where they left off when she sent him away. Only better, because now there was that fizzy, sparkly thing they had going, now that she had finally admitted that she wanted him for more than a friend.

After she put Ginny back to bed, she went out and sat with Gabe until the movie ended. Then he kissed her good-night, another deep, passionate, beautiful kiss.

When he lifted his head, she said, "I'll get you some blankets and a pillow."

"I can get them. Go on to bed."

She kissed him once more, because she could. Because it felt so very good. And finally, reluctantly, she left him to make his own bed.

Gabe set his BlackBerry to wake him at five-thirty.

Twice in the night, he heard Ginny crying. But before he could get up and go in to offer help, the crying would stop. He would drift off to sleep again.

In the morning, he woke before first light to the buzzing of the alarm. He'd slept in his clothes, so he didn't have to waste any time getting dressed. In his stocking feet, carrying his boots, he made a quick stop in the half bath across from the stairs and then, as silently as he could, went out the back door.

Mary woke at a little after six with a smile on her face. She took a quick shower and dressed, eager to get out to the living room—and Gabe.

But when she tiptoed out there, he was gone. Her heart sank that he'd left without a word. Until she opened the curtain and saw that his fancy car was still there.

The bathroom, then?

Two steps toward the stairs and she could see the half-bath door was open. No one in there. She went up the stairs. That bathroom was empty, too.

About then, she realized he must have gone outside. To tend the animals for her?

She smiled. How sweet.

She went out the back door to thank him with a good-morning kiss. He emerged from the barn before she got beyond the rusty ironwork posts that held up the patio cover.

She lingered there, waiting for him, her heart rising inside her chest. He came to her and she went eagerly into his arms.

After the kiss, he said, "I took care of the animals."

"I thought maybe you had. Thank you."

"And that guy you let sleep in the barn?"

She frowned up at him. Hadn't they put that issue to rest? "What about him?"

"He's okay. He helped me out with the horses and the goats. Name's Wyatt McCrae. Raised on a ranch down by Laredo. Been working cattle since he was a kid, but he's hit a patch of real bad luck…."

Where was this going? "I'll invite him in for breakfast, if that's what you're hinting at."

His gaze held hers. "He needs a job, Mary. And you need a hand. If you're serious about keeping this place, you've got to have someone to mend fences and burn ditches. Someone to whitewash the barn and slap a coat of paint on the house. You're a fine woman. Steady. Strong. But you've got your hands full, with Ginny and the writing you do."

"I know I need a hand. But I can't afford to hire anyone right now." It galled her to say it, though she had no doubt he knew it already.

"No problem. I'll pay his wages."

"Gabe. No. That's not right." She tried to pull away.

He wouldn't let go. "That's pride talking. The man needs a job. And you need a hand. And I'm willing to fork out the cash to give you both what you need. Let me do that, Mary. Just take a deep breath and say yes."

She looked in those blue eyes and thought how she trusted him. How it was a fine thing he wanted to do and she should be grateful instead of stiff with hurt pride. Mary took that deep breath. "All right. Go tell my new hand there'll be breakfast in twenty minutes."

At a little after seven, when he got ready to leave, Gabe felt pretty pleased with the way things were going.

It had been decided that Wyatt would take the cabin a couple hundred feet east of the barn. It had served as a bunkhouse decades ago, when the Lazy H was a going concern. The roof needed patching and things were pretty rustic inside, but Wyatt said he'd fix it up in his spare time. The electricity in there was working, and Mary would see about having the phone turned on again.

Over breakfast, Wyatt had said he had a knack with machinery. He was in the barn, trying to get Rowdy's old truck started, as Mary walked Gabe out to his car.

She kissed him goodbye, coming into his arms, fitting there just perfectly. The only bad thing about having Mary in his arms was that eventually he had to let her go.

And he did, with reluctance. He got in the Jag and rolled down the window and she bent close and kissed him once more.

"How many cars have you got, anyway?" she teased.

"Several. Kiss me again."

She did, her head halfway in the window. "Come back soon," she murmured when they came up for air.

"How about tonight?"

"That would be perfect."

"Seven o'clock?"

"It's a date."

From the barn around the back of the house came a grinding sound and then a couple of backfires.

Mary laughed. "That truck hasn't worked for as long as I can remember."

"I get the feeling Wyatt's not giving up till he makes it happen."

More grinding and backfires. And then they heard it— a ragged roar as the old engine came back to life.

"I don't believe it," said Mary. "Will miracles never cease?"

"Let's hope not. Tonight?"

"Tonight," she repeated softly, and stepped back from the car so he could drive away. He watched her in his rearview mirror. She was smiling, her arms wrapped around herself, her shiny hair blowing across her cheek. He wanted to back up and take her in his arms for one more kiss.

But he kept going. There would be plenty of time for kisses tonight and the next night. And the night after that.

He went to his place to clean up, and packed a bag while he was there, thinking he would head for Mary's straight from the office that evening. He'd be prepared if she let him spend another night on her couch. Funny how he'd rather sleep on Mary's sofa than in his own big, empty king-sized bed.

He took the Porsche 911 to BravoCorp. The hum of the powerful engine always soothed him. And the closer he got to the confrontation with his father, the edgier he felt.

There would be shouting. And probably threats. Gabe did have a plan.

He only hoped to hell it would work.

Chapter Eleven

As it turned out, Gabe didn't have to go looking for his father.

Georgia glanced up from her computer when he came in. "Davis just called. He wants you in his office right away."

So Gabe got back on the elevator and went up to the top floor. Davis's assistant sent him right in.

His father rose from his desk when he entered. "Gabe." He sounded affable. Even welcoming. "Great. Have a seat." He gestured at one of the leather chairs and Gabe took it. Davis sat back down, too. "I dropped by your place last night. But I missed you."

His father's sudden friendliness had the hairs on the back of Gabe's neck standing up. Since the argument Thursday before last, when Gabe had refused to hound Mary any further, Davis had been cool toward him at best, and even hostile more than once. Why the abrupt change of attitude?

"I'm surprised," Gabe said.

Davis tried to look innocent. "What? That I stopped in to see my own son?"

"Well, Dad. You and I haven't exactly been on good terms lately."

Davis cleared his throat. "Ahem. Well, yes. That's so. And I want to…get past that. Heal the breach between us. It's not good to let bad feelings fester. We are family, after all."

Gabe put it together. "You told Mom about it. Now she's after you to make it up with me."

"Ahem. Well. She's a wise woman, your mother."

"I'm more than willing to get straight with you," Gabe volunteered.

"Excellent." His father beamed. He reached a hand across the desk. Gabe took it and they shook. "Now." Davis settled back, elbows on the padded chair arms, big fingers laced over his belt. "Pack a bag. I'm sending you to California to meet with Jonas." Jonas Bravo was a second or third cousin—Gable could never remember which. The notorious Blake Bravo had been Jonas's uncle. And the Bravo Baby was Jonas's younger brother. Now and then, BravoCorp and Jonas did business. "You leave Thursday morning at 5:00 a.m., with Matt." Matt was the fourth born of Gabe's brothers. He was BravoCorp's CFO. "Jonas is offering us a piece of a wind-energy project he's developing. Hear his proposal, get specifics, see what you think. He sent a nice, fat file attachment containing the preliminary information. I sent it on to your in-box."

"I'll look it over."

"Good, then." Davis nodded. He looked supremely satisfied with himself. "We're back on track, the two of us.

And you're on board for the California trip. Anything else we need to discuss?"

"As a matter of fact, there is."

Davis dipped his head. "I'm listening."

Gabe laid it right out there. "I got a call from Mary Hofstetter yesterday evening. She asked to meet me so I went out to see her at the Lazy H. As it turned out, she'd just had a visit from Emily Gray."

Davis's steady gaze narrowed. "You were with the Hofstetter woman last night, then?"

"I was, but that's not my point. Emily Gray is an excellent negotiator. And smart. She would never make the mistake of stepping out of bounds without your specific instructions. So I have to believe that you're the one who told her to threaten Mary with 'unpleasant' consequences if she didn't get with the program and sell BravoCorp the Lazy H."

"Is there something going on between you and Mary Hofstetter?"

"Not the issue."

"It is as far as I'm concerned."

"Dad. Listen. No matter what you do, Mary is not selling her ranch. Give it up. Move on."

Davis's square jaw was set. "You know I want that land. The widow's in over her head, holding on to something she can't take care of. *I'll* make good use of that ranch and you know it."

"You're repeating yourself. And you're not getting that land. No matter what you do."

"We'll see about that."

Gabe pulled out the big guns. "Try anything illegal—burn her out or poison her well, whatever—and Mary will have me representing her in court."

Davis sat very still in his thronelike chair. "You wouldn't."

"I would. Maybe I wouldn't be able to prove you were behind whatever ugliness you're planning, but I can make you pay on other levels."

"Don't threaten me, Gabriel." His father's green eyes burned with fury. He didn't enjoy having his own tactics turned back on him.

Gabe replied flatly, "It's not a threat, Dad. It's a hard fact. It's not going to look good in the media, Bravo against Bravo."

Davis straightened his desk pad. Then, with a low sound of disgust, he pushed himself out of his big chair, turned and went to the window. He stared out at the city spread wide below him. "Your grandfather won Bravo Ridge on a bet," he said.

"I know, Dad."

"A horse race." Davis went on as if Gabe hadn't spoken. "Between Emilio Cabrera's best Andalusian and a fast little Mustang your grandfather found running wild and trained to the saddle himself. That Mustang won. And your grandfather took the last of the Cabrera holdings, their land and their hacienda that they called *La Joya*, the jewel, and renamed the whole thing Bravo Ridge after a clump of rocks he'd stood on when he first saw the Cabrera spread. We've had bad blood with the Cabreras ever since. They would never forgive us for stealing their heritage, for making it ours. But we did. Bravo Ridge was the start of it, of the Bravo dynasty in Texas...."

It was an old story and not a pretty one. The feud between the Bravos and the Cabreras continued to the present day. There had been blood spilled on both sides. Blood spilled and revenge taken.

Gabe would have told his father he didn't need to hear

it all again. But he kept silent. He had the sense Davis was working around to the current conflict between the two of them.

Davis said, "My father had seven sons and he chased all of them away. Except me. I was too mean to let him scare me off. And I swore I'd never drive my own kids away." Finally, he faced Gabe again. "I don't want this."

Relief washed through Gabe. He softened his tone. "I know you don't. Nobody does."

"Ash says he's got another property that will work as well or better. He wants me to go out and take a look at it." He slanted Gabe a careful glance. "*Are* you involved with the Hofstetter widow?"

Gabe refused to be deterred from the main point. "Dad." He spoke gently now. "You never could stand to be told 'no.' It's a character flaw. Ash won't steer you wrong. Go see the other property. Move on."

Davis returned to his chair. He settled back into it. And then, at last, he said the words Gabe was waiting to hear. "All right. We'll move on."

"Thank you."

His father gave a regal nod. "It's done. Now, about you and the widow…"

Gabe answered him honestly then. "I'm involved with Mary. And I like her. A lot. I…admire her. She's a special kind of woman, sweet and bright and good. And a straight talker, too."

Davis said nothing for several seconds. His expression was unreadable. But Gabe knew his father. Though Davis was less than pleased, he didn't want to alienate Gabe all over again. Not now, when they'd reached a shaky peace at last. So he was taking his time, trying to choose the right words.

In the end, he threw up both hands. "I've got to speak frankly. Even if your mother does have my hide for it."

Gabe braced himself. He really didn't want to listen to his father say things they would both regret. But he knew there was no stopping Davis now. He would have his say.

"Look, son. I believe in love and all that. Without your mother at my side, I would be nothing. But we both know you could have your pick of women from some of the best Texas families. Couldn't you just fall for one of them?"

Gabe almost smiled. "'Fraid it's more about the woman than the size of her fortune, Dad."

Davis swore under his breath. "First Ash and now you. Don't get me wrong. I love my daughter-in-law. Tessa's a fine woman. And she makes Ash happy. But isn't it enough that my oldest son married a shopkeeper from the wilds of California? Now *you're* getting involved with a dirt-poor rancher's widow? I've been counting on you to marry well when you finally decide to settle down."

Screw the fragile peace between them. Gabe wanted to pop his father a good one about then. He could punch the old man's lights out just in defense of Tessa, for starters. If not for Tessa, Ash would be dead. Plus, Tessa was an all-around good person. You'd think Davis would be grateful to see Ash married to a woman like her.

But no. He was miffed because she lacked important family connections and a fat fortune.

And on top of talking trash about Tessa, Davis had the nerve to get on Gabe about seeing Mary.

Mary. Gabe saw her pretty face in his mind's eye. Yeah, he was wild for Mary, all right. He wanted to do whatever he could for her, to spend every spare minute in her company. He had no idea where this thing with them was going.

But his dad could have saved his breath. Marriage wasn't an issue. In the end, Gabe just wasn't the marrying kind—not that it was any of Davis's business, either way.

And he'd been silent too long. His father prompted, "Gabe? What? Now I've offended you again?"

You damn well have, he thought. In a too-quiet voice, he said, "Mary and I haven't come to the settling-down point. But if that happened, I would be honored to be the husband of such a fine woman." It was the truth, as far as it went. He looked his dad dead in the eye.

Davis glanced away first. Gabe had been reasonably sure that he would. Davis Bravo could be pigheaded, heavy-handed and overbearing. But he had one saving grace. He loved his family. His wife and his children were everything to him. He'd already said it a few minutes ago: In the end, he would never drive any one of his sons or daughters away.

"All right," said Davis, sounding weary. "I guess I went a little too far. And I apologize for any out-of-line remarks I made about the widow."

"Her name is Mary."

"Ahem. Yes. Mary. I apologize for anything I said about Mary—and you'd damn well better be satisfied now, Gabe. I'm giving up on the Lazy H. And now you've got my solemn word I'll be staying out of your love life, too."

Gabe gave him a slow smile. "It's a moment to savor, Dad."

"Glad you're enjoying yourself." Davis glanced at the blinking light on his phone. "I want to take this call. Anything else?"

"No. I think we're finished here."

* * *

Mary was waiting for him out on the porch, perched on the top step, when he drove up that evening.

She rose to greet him, her eyes bright as stars. "I fed Wyatt. He's gone to the cabin for the night. And Ginny just fell asleep."

He pulled her close. The kiss they shared curled his toes inside his boots. When they came up for air, he asked, "You save any dinner for me?"

"Right this way."

He ate the fried chicken and mashed potatoes she put in front of him while she told him how hard Wyatt had worked all day. "He fixed the fence around the goat yard."

"That's great." When goats got loose, they ate everything in sight—laundry off a clothesline. Tack, if you let them. They'd happily chew a man's saddle and bridle to bits.

Mary added, "He wants to fix up their yard a little, build a new goat house, stuff like that. And he wants to build a better lean-to for the horses, keep them more comfortable when the weather's bad."

"Glad to hear Wyatt's working out."

"Oh, Gabe. I think he is. Thank you for hiring him."

He saved the news of Davis's change of heart for later, when he had her under him on the sofa and they were making out like a couple of teenagers.

They'd been kissing for maybe five minutes straight without coming up for air when he lifted his head and said, "Guess what?"

She gazed up at him, her eyes glowing with arousal, and he wondered how he was going to last four more weeks without scooping her up and carrying her to bed. "No idea," she whispered. "But tell me later. Right now, you should kiss me…" She wrapped her hand around his neck and drew him down to her again.

He kissed her. At length. And the next time he lifted his mouth from hers, he said, "It's handled. BravoCorp will find the land they need elsewhere."

"Um…" She started to pull him close again. And then his words finally registered. Her lazy-lidded gaze widened. "Did you just say what I thought you said?"

"Uh-huh."

"Seriously? No more visits from Emily Gray?"

"Or any other BravoCorp representatives. Never again."

"No more talk of how 'unpleasant' things are going to get?"

"Put all that behind you. It's over. Done. I talked to my father this morning. He can be a sonofagun. But when he gives his word, it's golden."

"And he gave his word today?"

"Yeah. He did."

She let out a whoop loud enough to wake the dead down in Mexico. "Get up."

"Huh?"

"Get off me." She gave a shove and he levered back on his knees. Swinging her bare feet to the floor, she leapt upright. Then, laughing, she grabbed his hand and pulled him up with her. "Dance with me."

"You want it, you got it." He grabbed her close and waltzed her around the room while her dog sat in the corner, watching with her ears perked. Mary stopped him in the archway to the kitchen. Swaying in his arms, she lifted on tiptoe and planted a big wet one square on his mouth.

"Gabe Bravo, you're a miracle worker."

"So I've been told."

"I have so many things to thank you for, it's getting embarrassing, not to mention repetitious. I'll never be able to pay you back."

Shamelessly, he took advantage of her gratitude. "I know one thing you could do…."

"Name it."

"I brought a bag. It's in the car. Let me stay overnight."

"Oh, Gabe…"

He realized she thought he meant in her bed. "Mary. Come on. I wouldn't do that to you. I meant on the couch."

Her sweet mouth formed a round O. "Well, all right." She laughed again. "I have to tell you. I don't get the appeal of that sofa. I know you've probably got a perfectly wonderful bed at home, big as a dance floor with a mattress like a cloud."

"I like it here. It's…comfortable here. Feels like home, you know?"

Her eyes shone with pleasure. "Like home, huh?"

"That's what I said."

"Be my guest, then. For tonight and tomorrow night— any night you please."

"That's another thing…" He guided a few stray strands of hair out of her eyes. How many times had he wanted to do that, to touch her in such a casual, intimate way?

Too many. And now, at last, he could.

A sweet smile bloomed. "What other thing?"

"I've got to fly to California on business. I'm leaving Thursday, before dawn."

She lifted on tiptoe again to brush a kiss across his lips. "I miss you already. How long will you be gone?"

"Probably till Monday. You think you'll be able to get along without me for four or five days?"

"It'll be tough. But somehow, I'll manage."

"I was thinking when I get back, we should go out someplace nice."

"A date? As in dinner and a movie?"

"Yeah. What do you say?"

"A date…" She seemed kind of taken with the idea. "Just you and me, out someplace with candles on the table, maybe, and a white tablecloth."

"A week from Friday? You think you can get Ida to babysit?"

"I'll ask her tomorrow. Right now, though, take me back to the sofa. Kiss me some more."

Mary did miss him when he left. So much. All out of proportion to how long he planned to be gone. She took comfort in the thought that it wasn't like when she'd sent him away after Ginny's birth.

This time, she wasn't losing him. This time, he would return to her in only a few days.

He surprised her on Sunday—which was Easter— showing up late in the afternoon, driving one of his sports cars. She heard an engine out in front and went to see who it was just as he emerged from the low, sleek car. He looked so handsome that her breath tangled in her throat and her heart turned over in her chest.

With a cry of pure joy, she ran out to meet him.

He paused halfway up the front walk, a slow smile curving his mouth, as she banged through the storm door. She raced down the steps and threw herself into his open arms.

"Happy to see me, huh?" Those unforgettable blue eyes gleamed down at her.

"Oh, yes. I am…"

He took her by the waist and lifted her high, letting her

slide down his strong, hard body, finally catching her mouth, kissing her.

Oh, the feel of his kisses. Nothing like them. Not ever, in the whole, wide world.

Inside, he held Ginny while Mary finished preparing Easter dinner. Ida came to eat with them. And Wyatt, of course. And Garland, too. The whole table seemed to have a glow about it to Mary. No holiday dinner ever tasted so good.

After the meal, they all went out and admired the way Wyatt had cleaned up the barn. He'd even swamped out the chicken coop.

Wyatt took Garland and Ida for a spin in the old Ford pickup. Ida came back laughing, swearing how she'd always hated that pickup. Rowdy's father was forever out tinkering with it when he wasn't mending fences or taking care of the livestock. He never seemed to have time to pay any attention to her.

"Not only was I stuck on this ranch," she said, "but my husband loved his pickup more than me." She slapped the old truck's rusted fender. "But you know, since this old hunk of junk and me are no longer in competition for my husband's affection, I've become kind of fond of her. Glad to see someone's got her working again."

Wyatt's ears were red with pleasured embarrassment. He kicked the dirt and said it wasn't any big deal.

Later, after everyone left, when Mary and Gabe were alone, she told him she'd given Wyatt the old truck. "I've been trying to get someone to come and haul it off since Rowdy died," she told him. "So it's not like I've been having trouble getting along without it."

"It's good," Gabe agreed. "To give Wyatt his own wheels.

Not only to work around the ranch, but also because a man needs the means to get where he's going."

She teased him about all of his cars then. And then he kissed her. And she forgot everything but the feel of his mouth on hers.

Friday night he took her to a beautiful restaurant overlooking the Riverwalk. There were white tablecloths and flowers on their table. And white candles, too. It was just as she'd imagined it. Magical. Romantic. Gabe wore a suit that probably cost a fortune. Mary thought she looked pretty good, too, in a sleeveless silk dress she'd found at a consignment shop when Ida took her and Ginny into San Antonio the day before so Mary could get her hair cut. The dress clung to her curves, and was a beautiful bronze color, with a sheen of gold or red, depending on how the light touched it. It made her look sophisticated, Ida had said.

Gabe told her she was beautiful and she *felt* beautiful. The evening was like a dream. The chef came out and talked to them, deferential to Gabe, suggesting a few menu choices they might enjoy.

As they lingered over a fabulous dessert of raspberries and lemon curd, a couple of sharp-dressed men about Gabe's age approached their table.

"Gabe. How's it been going?"

There was hand-shaking and introductions. Mary felt both men's eyes on her when they thought she wasn't looking, probably assuming she was just another conquest of the Bravo Bachelor. Mary grinned to herself. Well, and she was, wasn't she?

Even if she couldn't help hoping what she shared with Gabe would end up being so much more.

"What was that secret smile about?" he asked, when the men had moved on.

She only shrugged and took another bite of that scrumptious dessert.

They went to his place after. It was gorgeous and ultra-modern. Mary thought it looked a little bit sterile, though. No wonder he preferred to stay at her place where it was homey, if not nearly as beautiful.

She drank mineral water and he had a beer and they kissed until steam was coming out of their ears. Sheesh. They'd be lucky if they both didn't explode before she got the approval for lovemaking from Dr. Breitmann.

Two weeks and three days. It wasn't *that* long…

At eleven, she had him take her home. She'd used a breast pump before he came to pick her up. But the way his kisses excited her, well…

If she didn't get home to her baby soon, she would be leaking all over her pretty silk dress—not that she told Gabe that. Some things a man just doesn't need to know. Not on a fabulous, romantic evening, anyway. Not on their first real date.

At her house, she thanked Ida and sent her home. She nursed Ginny and put her back to bed. Then she and Gabe went out to the patio together. They sat in the plastic chairs and looked at the stars.

He slept on her sofa that night. And the night after that. And every night his work allowed it.

Mary treasured each moment she spent at his side. She longed for the six weeks to hurry up and be over so she could belong to him in every way.

Sometimes, she would think of Rowdy. And miss him. And even talk to him on occasion when she and Ginny were alone in the house, talk to him as if he were there with her, still at her side. But she didn't long for him the way she used to, she didn't feel that hurtful sadness to have lost him.

Now the sadness was gentle. And sweet. Now she had Gabe. Love had found her again.

Love.

Oh, yes. It had happened. Mary was in love again and the one she loved was Gabe.

No, she didn't tell him. It felt to her that it would be rushing things a little to start defining what they had together so soon. To call it love outright. Out loud.

No. Not yet. She just wanted to be with him, whenever he came to her.

They went out again the next weekend. On Saturday, to a fun Mexican place Gabe liked. And afterwards, they went dancing. Mary had a ball.

That night, when they got home to the Lazy H, after Ida left, another guy without a place to stay knocked on the door. Mary gave him some leftover chicken and he slept in the barn.

The next morning, before dawn, Gabe went out to talk to him and hired him to work with Wyatt. His name was Ty Grimes.

Ty came in for breakfast. He was a soft-spoken fellow in his mid-twenties. He knew ranch work, he said. He'd run cattle and even herded sheep. Plus, he'd worked for a plumber once. And an electrical contractor. He was handy, he said, with a hammer and nail. He and Wyatt seemed to get along.

After Ty and Wyatt finished the meal and left them alone, Mary turned to Gabe. "Okay. Two hands. I can use them."

"I know you can."

"I might be able to make a little time to plant a garden one of these days, since Wyatt and Ty will be taking care of most everything else."

"Great idea."

"And I've been thinking about expanding my goat operation."

"You've got five goats, Mary. That's hardly an operation."

"Well, and that's my point. I hate selling off the kids. But I've been doing it because I can't handle any more of them. Now, though, since they *are* milk goats, maybe we could start selling the milk, start making goat cheese. I know, it gets complicated. Permits, special equipment. I don't want to discount any possibilities, though."

"Good thinking."

"But, Gabe, two hands is enough. Please. No more."

He grinned. "What? You want me to promise?"

"I do. Absolutely. Promise you won't hire me any more hands."

"What will you do for me if I promise?"

"Gabe Bravo. You really have to try and think of other things besides sex."

"I'm trying. Believe me. It's just not working very well."

"Eight days," she said softly.

He reached across the table. She reached, too. Their hands met in the middle.

The next week, Gabe was gone to California Tuesday through Saturday morning, wrapping up the details of a wind-energy deal. Saturday night he showed up at her door with a gorgeous diamond tennis bracelet and a platinum necklace with a diamond pendant to match.

She told him it was too much.

And he looked bewildered. "What? You don't like diamonds?"

"Of course I like diamonds." She touched the chain around her neck, gazed down at the sparkly bracelet adorning her arm. "But you've done enough for me. Too much, really…"

"I like to do things for you." He wrapped his arms around her and kissed her slow and deep. And when he lifted his head, he grabbed her hand. "Come on out to the car. I bought a few things for Ginny."

It turned out he'd gone shopping with Emma Bravo, the wife of the distant Bravo cousin who had offered Bravo-Corp a cut of the wind-energy deal. Emma was from Texas, too. And she'd had all kinds of suggestions as to what to buy a baby girl. She and Gabe must have cleaned out every pricey baby boutique in Beverly Hills. There were twenty-three darling little outfits. And a top-of-the-line stroller and baby toys for days.

"Gabe, you'll spoil her completely."

"She's a baby. You can't spoil a baby…."

"I mean it, Gabe. This is way too much."

"Come on, let's get all this stuff inside."

Mary knew she had to make it clear to him, had to firmly draw the line. He was paying the wages of two ranch hands for her, for heaven's sake. That was more than enough—too much, really. The diamonds and the carload of baby things? He was getting way beyond it.

But he looked so happy to be showering her and her baby with gifts, it seemed kind of small of her not to simply be grateful and leave it at that. So she thanked him and kissed him and let it go.

Sunday Donna Lynn had a barbecue at her place. There

were several older people there—Donna Lynn and her husband, Ida and some of their mutual friends. And Donna Lynn had four daughters, each of them married with kids. So there were people Mary and Gabe's age, too, and a whole bunch of little ones running everywhere.

They all made a big deal about Ginny. And Gabe fit right in—but then, he could fit in anywhere, it seemed to Mary. He always knew the right thing to say and he seemed to have a good time whether he was holding Ginny on his arm to quiet her when she was colicky, or jetting off to California to firm up a business deal. He could go anywhere and be liked and included.

And boy, was she over the moon about him or what?

Sometimes she did wonder where, exactly, they were going together: a rich bachelor and a hardworking ranch widow with a baby to care for. Seriously. Where could it go between them?

And then she would chide herself for worrying about nothing. Yes, they had their separate lives. But when they were together—and they were together often—it was magic. She needed to focus on the magic and stop wondering how it would all work out in the end.

At last, the big day came. She went to see Dr. Breitmann. He gave the okay. No more having to put the brakes on at the most intimate moments. Tonight, for the first time, she and Gabe could follow the mood wherever it took them.

She had been looking forward to this day for weeks.

And halfway back to the ranch, she realized she was terrified.

Chapter Twelve

Mary could hardly believe her own reaction.

She was a grown woman, for heaven's sake. A grown woman who'd been married and had a child. Still, she felt like a virgin all over again. And not in a sexy, Madonna-like way. She almost missed the turn to the house, she was so busy obsessing over how it was really going to happen now. She would be naked in a bed with Gabe.

Would he find her too naïve? He'd been with so many gorgeous, sophisticated women. Mary just…wasn't. Not gorgeous. And certainly not sophisticated.

They'd been waiting so long for the go-ahead, the anticipation building. Would the actual…event be a letdown?

And what about her body? It shouldn't matter, she knew that. When you cared for someone, it should be about who they were, as a person. Not how they looked without their clothes. But the hard fact remained. She wasn't as slim as she'd been before Ginny. Her tummy wasn't exactly flat anymore.

Oh, dear Lord…

She was being completely silly. She had to snap out of it. Gabe had seen her give birth, for heaven's sake. She didn't think twice if he was sitting there next to her when she nursed Ginny.

But still. She couldn't help it. She was scared. She worried that she would disappoint him, somehow. Worried that, after all the weeks of waiting, the reality couldn't possibly stack up to the fantasy.

He called at five. When she answered, the first thing he said was, "Are you okay?" The question didn't surprise her. She'd promised him yesterday that she would call him the minute she left Dr. Breitmann's office.

And she should have. She *would* have. If only she hadn't discovered she was scared spitless of the night to come. "I know I should have called…."

"Mary. Is something the matter?" He sounded worried.

And she felt defensive—and guilty for causing him pointless concern. "I'm fine. Honestly. Everything's…good. In working order, if you know what I mean."

He was silent. Then, cautiously, he asked, "Did I do something?"

"What are you talking about?"

"Did I do something to make you mad?"

"Mad? I'm not mad."

"Mary, come on. What the hell's going on?"

"Nothing. Not a thing. I bought condoms because, well, the birth control pills take a month before you can count on them."

"Mary."

"What?"

"Are you scared?"

She almost laughed. It would have been a panicked, frantic sound. Somehow, she swallowed it down. And baldly lied. "Scared. Me? No, of course not."

"You're scared."

She blew out a hard breath. "Well, all right. A little—or maybe, a lot."

"Don't be."

"Easy for you to say."

Another silence, then, "Why do I get the feeling that whatever I say next is going to be the wrong thing?"

"Sorry. Truly. I'm being an idiot and I know it—and yet I don't seem to be able to stop. Which only makes it all even worse."

Cautiously, he suggested, "Seven, then?"

"Seven."

Mary fed the hands early. Then she took a long, hot bath. She shaved. Extensively. She got out of the tub and slathered on lotion and then just stood there for much too long, staring at herself in the steamy bathroom mirror, wishing she wasn't so nervous, almost wanting to call Gabe back and tell him not to come over, after all. That they could do this some other time. Maybe next year.

But she didn't call him. She put fresh sheets on the bed, folding them back, plumping the pillows. She even set the box of condoms on the nightstand within easy reach, and then stood there, arms wrapped around herself, staring at that box.

Could this really be happening?

She fed the dog. When Ginny started fussing, she fed her and changed her. Then she moved her bassinet out to the kitchen. It just seemed strange to think of being intimate with Gabe while the baby was in the room.

When she heard his car pull up, right on time, she was nothing short of a nervous wreck. She stood in the middle of the living room, wanting to run out and greet him on the front step, while at the same time longing to spin on her heel, race up the stairs and hide in the closet of the spare bedroom.

She heard his boots on the steps and forced herself to move forward, to cover the distance to the door, to pull it wide and push open the storm door.

Flowers. He had flowers. A big, gorgeous bouquet of pink lilies and blue irises. He said her name, "Mary." And the look in his eyes said he wanted to kiss her. And more. A whole lot more. A slow shudder ran through her. It was partly nerves.

And partly a sudden, weak, lovely feeling of arousal. To have his hands on her, all over her. To not have to stop this time…

For a moment, she knew it would all be okay. Better than okay. And then her fear rose up again. She swallowed, convulsively.

He held out the flowers.

She took them. "Oh, Gabe…"

"Better put them in water."

"Uh. Yes. Of course…" She stepped back and he came inside. She got the faintest whiff of that great aftershave he wore. And she wanted to reach for him, as she would have any other evening.

Reach for him and lift her mouth for his kiss.

But if she did that, anything might happen. She whirled and headed for the kitchen as he bent to greet Brownie. "I'll just…a vase. I'll get a vase."

Once he'd petted the dog, he followed behind her. She could feel him there, feel his eyes on her. She'd worn snug jeans and a plain white shirt. Kind of keeping it simple, trying not to make a big deal of it.

Which was totally ridiculous. She *was* making a big deal of it. She was making a huge, impossible deal.

The crystal vase that had belonged to her mom was up on the top shelf of a cabinet. She got the footstool.

Gabe said, "Here, I'll get it."

"No. It's fine. I can do it."

They were whispering, in order not to wake Ginny, who slept in her bassinet on the far side of the table. Mary got up there and got down the vase, almost dropping it in her numb-fingered nervousness. But in the end, she got it down safely and filled it with water and put the flowers in it, taking a moment to arrange them a little at the counter, to make a nice display.

When she turned and set the vase on the table, she found Gabe watching her. Heat rose within her again. She felt a flush flooding upward, over her throat to her cheeks, and had to resist the urge to put her hands against her face to cool it.

Unable to hold his gaze, she slid her eyes away and stepped back from the table.

"They look nice," she whispered.

"Beautiful," he whispered back.

She knew he wasn't talking about the flowers. "Um. Have you eaten? I can—"

"Mary." Just that. Just her name in a whisper.

She met his eyes again. She couldn't speak. She looked away, anywhere but at him—at the door to the patio, at the bassinet with her sleeping baby in it, down at her Keds...

And then he moved. He came to her. He was beside her,

touching her shoulder, urging her with just a brush of his hand to turn toward him. He put a finger under her chin, the light, warm touch making her shiver with mingled fear and a sudden, bone-melting surge of anticipation. He guided her face up.

"It's okay," he whispered.

And then, light as a breath, his lips touched hers—just that, a touch, no more. He lifted his mouth away from hers. And he waited, his eyes sapphire blue, soft with emotion. And male intent.

That strange, lazy feeling of arousal flowed through her again. She looked up at his beautiful mouth, at those eyes that promised a passion she'd never known before.

She couldn't stand it. With a low moan, she surged up, wrapping her arms around his neck, pulling him down to her, pressing her mouth, hard, to his.

Chapter Thirteen

In the middle of that hungry, thrilling kiss, he swept her up into his arms, the move so smooth and sudden, she gasped.

He pulled his lips from hers enough to whisper, "You're safe. I have you…."

And then he kissed her again. She gave in to that kiss, she let go of her fear and allowed desire to take her, sighing against his parted lips as he carried her around the table and to the bedroom, pausing just beyond the threshold to push the door shut with his boot.

He let her down beside the bed. "Mary…" He unbuttoned her shirt, his long, strong fingers quick and skilled. She tried not to wonder how many other women's shirts he might have undone for them. She tried not to think at all.

It worked. More or less. She *was* excited. Her pulse turned to a throb, slow and thick and hungry. He took the sides of her shirt and peeled them open.

And he bent close, kissed her, at the tender groove in the base of her throat, and lower, in the cove between her breasts.

The shirt dropped away. Mary shut her eyes. It was easier not to look. To lose herself in the tender brush of his hands as they glided to her shoulders, hooking the straps of her bra, guiding them down her arms.

He reached behind her without her even really knowing he was doing that—until her bra fell loose from her rib cage. He whisked it away before she could grab it back and hug it tight against herself.

She was bare from the waist up.

"So pretty…" His hand cupped her right breast.

She gasped and caught his wrist. "Careful…" She didn't know how to say it, to tell him that her milk might come.

But he seemed to understand. He made a low, gentle sound deep in his throat, a sound meant to soothe. And then he touched her throat, smoothed her hair back away from her shoulder, caught her earlobe between thumb and fore-finger and worried it gently.

Heat shot through her as he rubbed her earlobe, like little jolts of lightning from where he touched her, down her neck, through the center of her to her core. Crazy, that such a small thing could excite her so completely.

She swayed against him. And he took her mouth again, kissing her deeply, as he worked the button at the top of her jeans and then slipped her zipper down with a soft hiss of sound.

He eased her jeans off, her panties with them. Every-thing pooled at her ankles. Her shoes were in the way.

Gabe took her bare waist and guided her down. She sat on the bed, her eyes still tightly shut, as she lost herself in the hot caress of his lips on hers.

He knelt before her. She felt him there, touching her calf, lifting her legs up—one and then the other—taking her Keds away, too. The jeans and panties followed. She heard a rustle of fabric and the soft thud of her shoes as he dropped them on the floor, out of the way.

"Mary…" His palms curved around the backs of her ankles, sliding up, sending hot shivers all through her. He cupped the tender grooves behind her knees. And he bent closer.

She sucked in a sharp breath and let it out on a slow sigh as he kissed her knees, first the left and then the right, pressing his lips against the round, hard shape of her knee bones, then sticking out his tongue and licking the places he had kissed.

Mary moaned. And she shuddered. He guided her knees apart.

She lifted a hand, touched his silky hair, threading her fingers through the strands, whispering things, wordless, breathless things, as he kissed the insides of her knees.

He urged her knees wider. She knew she was totally revealed to him then. Her most secret place, wet now, and yearning. Wanting him. His touch. His caress. And more.

Everything.

All of him.

"Beautiful…" His voice drifted to her, low and rough with desire.

And his hands, fingers spread, glided along the tops of her thighs, a long, slow caress that had her holding her breath, waiting. Yearning. Burning for what would come next.

And then he touched her—there, where she wanted him. Where she needed him. His warm fingers parted her, one slipping inside.

And then two.

With his other hand, he found the heart of her pleasure. When he touched her there, she braced her hands behind her and let her head drop back. She cried out low and hungrily. And then he moved forward, shifting even closer. He put his mouth there....

Oh, never. Never, ever had she felt such wonder as that. She sighed and let go. She lay back across the bed with a shuddering moan as he kissed her there, endlessly, deeply, as if he would never stop. And as he tasted her in that most intimate way, his fingers stroked her.

Mary moaned and tossed her head against the sheet and wondered how she could have been afraid of this beauty, this glory, this lovely shimmering that started where he kissed her and spread out, racing along every eager, singing nerve.

He kept kissing her, kept touching her with those knowing fingers of his, kept stroking her, playing her body, making her sigh and moan and move her hips. She reached out to the side, her hands sliding on the cool sheets, gripping. Releasing. Gripping again.

It went on forever. She gloried in it. She never, ever wanted him to stop.

But something was building, growing, gathering tight.

And then opening wide as she moved against the wet press of his mouth.

Mary cried out as her climax shuddered through her, taking her up so high and spilling her over a waterfall of pleasure into a lazy pool of fulfillment.

She sighed and went lax, her fingers loosening their tight grip on the sheet, slowly letting go. He kept kissing her until she couldn't bear it anymore. It was simply more stimulation than she could take right then. She moaned and pushed at his shoulders.

And he pulled away. As soon as she lost the touch of his mouth, she wanted him back again. She smiled to herself at her own contrariness—and sighed at the wonder of what had just happened. She felt the air of the room against her wetness, cool and soothing.

After a moment of pleasant drifting, she opened her eyes for the first time since he'd carried her in there and set her on the floor by the bed.

He sat back on his knees, his hands on her thighs, his mouth red and swollen from the oh-so-arousing things he had done to her.

His smile was slow and achingly sweet. "See? Not so scary, after all."

"Oh, Gabe. It was…just wonderful. Amazing. Perfect." She reached down her hands for him.

"What?" he asked, that smile of his telling her he already knew.

Huskily, she commanded, "Come here…"

And he did. He rocked back onto his heels and rose to join her on the bed, stretching out with his boots over the edge, wrapping her close in his arms. He was still fully dressed.

She, on the other hand, was stark naked.

An hour ago, she never would have believed she would be lying here now, held tight in his embrace, without so much as a sheet to cover her. Yet here she was, feeling absolutely terrific. Feeling free. Feeling totally satisfied.

She laughed low in her throat and cuddled closer to him. He stroked her hair. She felt his lips, warm and so good, as he pressed a kiss at the crown of her head.

And there was more. He pushed his hips against her and

she felt his heat, the ridge of his arousal, hard and ready, through his clothes. Satisfaction made her bold. She slid a hand down between their bodies and touched him, cupping her fingers around him, lengthwise. He groaned in response and moved against her palm.

"Oh, Gabe. I…" *Love you.* She almost said it. But something made her hold back, some sense that he wasn't ready to hear it, that he might never be. And *she* wasn't ready to know that about him.

He didn't seem to mind, or even notice, the words she hadn't said. He stroked her shoulder, ran warm, knowing fingers down the bumps of her spine, fingers that spread wide as he got lower, cupping her bottom, bringing her in even closer than before.

Her fears, by then, hardly more a distant memory, she edged her thumb under the fly of his pants and found the zipper tab. Slowly, she brought it down.

He went very still then. A breath-held kind of stillness.

With a secret smile of womanly power, she eased her hand inside. He groaned at that, and took her mouth in a penetrating kiss, his tongue sweeping in, seeking and claiming the wet surfaces beyond her lips.

Mary kissed him back, with all the heat and passion she possessed. She kissed him back, her fingers finding the second fly in the front of his boxers and sliding through.

She touched him and he moaned into her mouth, a sound that encouraged her, a sound that begged her not to stop. She didn't stop. Oh, no. She wrapped her fingers tight around his hard, hot length.

He groaned then, a deeper sound than before, a sound of surrender. And she stroked him, slowly.

But his pants and his boxers were in the way. She

wanted them gone. She eased her hand free—and he grabbed her wrist. He groaned his need into her mouth. He didn't want her to let go.

But then she showed him that she only meant to undo the button at the top of his zipper, to spread his fly wide for better access. He stopped fighting her then.

He kissed her and she touched him under the silky cover of his boxers, taking him in her grip, stroking him, circling the silky head, grasping the shaft, moving smoothly down to the base and up again.

He felt so hot and satiny. She couldn't resist. She eased his boxers out of the way. He lifted up enough that she could push everything down around his thighs.

And then she had him. All of him. She broke the endless kiss they shared and sought his eyes. He met her gaze, his eyes like oceans, so blue. So deep….

And then she lowered her head to him. She took his heat and hardness into her mouth. He threaded his fingers into her hair, holding her, steadying and guiding her, as she took him deep and slowly released him. Oh, the sounds of pleasure he made then.

By that time, it seemed impossible that she had ever been scared of this—of them, together, in this most intimate way. Impossible. There was absolutely nothing to be scared of.

There was only pleasure. Only this wonderful man, the man she loved, only the touch of him, the feel of him, the taste of him in her mouth, on her tongue…

She wanted to take him all the way, as he had done for her. But he wouldn't allow it.

"Not yet. Mary, wait…" He pulled back. But only long enough to get out of his boots, rip off his shirt and shove his pants and boxers off. He tossed them over the end of the bed. "Condoms?" He groaned the word.

She pointed to the box, right there in plain sight on the nightstand. He reached for it, had one out and rolled down over him in seconds flat. And then he pulled her close again, rolling with her, until he was on top and he could ease her knees apart.

Settling between her open thighs, he braced himself up on his hands, the lean muscles in his arms knotting tight. She reached up, took his face between her hands, pulled him down for a kiss as she felt him, smooth and hard, nudging her secret flesh, there, where she wanted him most.

He pressed in. She kissed him, sighing into his mouth, raising her legs and wrapping them around him, pulling him into her.

All the way. So deep. So exactly right.

He rocked against her and she responded, kissing him deeply as he rode her. She moved with him. It was effortless. Magical. Exactly as she had dreamed it might be in her wildest fantasies. And better.

Oh, yes. Better…

She pulled him down onto her so she could feel him fully, the thrilling male weight of him, heavy on top of her, pressing her into the mattress. He lifted his mouth once, breaking the endless kiss, but only long enough to whisper her name. "Mary…"

And she gave his back to him. "Gabe…"

And then she was reaching for the finish again, hitting the top—and hovering there, above the world, above everything. Until the sweet tension burst wide open and she was falling softly into fulfillment, a long, slow, delicious glide.

He came, then, right after she did. And her body, acutely

sensitized to pleasure at that point, responded. She hit the peak all over again, a shattering fulfillment, as he pulsed deep within her.

She clutched him, hard and tight, and she cried out his name, thinking *I love you, Gabe. You are my love…*

But no. She didn't say her love out loud. Even in her ecstasy, she kept it back.

They slept together that night, in her bed.

And the next night, when he came to her, he brought her a necklace, her birthstone—a sapphire—ringed with diamonds on a delicate gold chain. She told him he had to stop buying her things.

He only laughed and kissed her. And then he scooped her up and carried her into the bedroom. They were in bed most of the night, except when they had to get up to take care of the baby. In bed, but rarely sleeping.

It was the same the next night. And the night after that. Unless his work took him away from her, he slept in her bed every night. They were so lovely, those nights. The best she had ever known.

The days were happy, too. And productive. Mary had her writing and her baby. And Wyatt and Ty were the greatest. They worked hard. They painted the exterior of the house, built a lean-to for the horses and a big, new goat house.

Gabe wanted them to put new roofs on the barn and the house, but Mary nixed that as too expensive. Gabe said he would be happy to pay for it. Mary just shook her head. As if he hadn't paid for way too much already.

Ty and Wyatt spent most mornings clearing brush. It was a tough, time-consuming job, since much of the land had become dangerously overgrown in recent years. Rowdy had loved his ranch, but he'd made his living working with Ida in town. And Mary had her writing to do. There had never been much time for the upkeep the land required.

That was all changed now. Thanks to Ty and Wyatt. And Gabe, most of all. Mary was so grateful to him. And so in love with him—more each day, it seemed to her.

She longed to know if he might love her, too. He certainly behaved as though he did. He was attentive. He made beautiful, passionate love to her. He came to her nearly every night. She had no doubt he was true to her.

Mary considered herself a practical and reasonable person. She did see how *un*reasonable it was of her to keep waiting for him to declare his love first. This was the twenty-first century, after all. Women didn't wait around anymore for things to happen *to* them. Women were empowered. They *made* things happen for themselves.

So on the last night of April, when Gabe arrived at her door, Mary put her fears of rejection aside. She sat him down on the sofa and told him she had something she needed to say.

Apparently, she hadn't put her fears away completely. He picked up on them and that scared *him*. "Mary. What? Damn it, what's wrong?"

Her heart was bouncing around like a jackrabbit on the run from a big, bad wolf. "I…um…"

He took her hand. "What's happened? You're white as a sheet. Tell me. Let me help."

Her hand felt clammy. She pulled it free of his. "I, um…"

"What? Say it."

Sheesh. She *was* empowered. She knew that. So why didn't she feel that way? "Um, I…"

He swore, reached for her—and let his hand drop when she shrank away. "My God. You're pregnant."

"No! Really. No…"

"Dying of some incurable disease."

"No."

"It's Ginny, right?" He whipped his head around toward the stairs. Mary had moved the baby up to her own room a week before. "Something's happened to—"

"No. Honestly. Ginny's fine."

"Damn it, Mary." He dragged his hands down his face. "You're killing me here. Whatever it is, will you just, please, say it?"

"Oh, God. Yes. All right." She sucked in a mammoth breath and used it to push the words out. "I…I love you, Gabe."

He gaped. "You love me."

She swallowed hard and sat up tall. "I do. Yes. I love you."

"And that's…it? That's all?"

She wanted to grab the *Ranch Life* magazine on the coffee table, roll it up and bop him on the head with it. Hard. "What do you mean, *that's all?* For me, it's important. For me, it's pretty huge." She strove for a reasonable tone. Because she was a reasonable person—and because she was right on the brink of jumping up, running into the bedroom, slamming the door, throwing herself on the bed and sobbing like a baby—which wouldn't be reasonable at all.

"Mary." Gabe took her hand again, his expression contrite. She didn't pull away that time, though she was seriously tempted to. "I'm sorry. I'm an ass."

She sniffed. "Well, yeah. That word crossed my mind. Among others…"

"Mary."

"What now?"

"I love you, too."

Too little, too late, she thought. "I'll bet you say that to all your girlfriends."

"No. I swear to you. I've never told a woman I loved her before now."

She slanted him a doubting look. "Never?"

"I swear. Never. Unless you count Gladys Dilly, in eighth grade. I really did think I loved Gladys. But, sadly, she dumped me during Christmas vacation for a band geek."

She stared at him. Hard. "You're serious?"

"Oh, yeah. His name was Dirk Smith. Played the tuba."

"Gabe. Stop."

He had the grace to look abashed. "Sorry. Just trying to lighten the mood. As a rule, I like to keep my relationships…open-ended."

She shook her head. "Makes it easier to escape when you're ready to go, right?"

"You know, it sounds pretty bad when you put it that way."

"But that doesn't make it any less true."

He looked at her levelly then. "It's different with you, Mary. I promise you. I'm crazy for you. Whatever you want from me, you can have it. Just ask."

He really did seem to mean it. And then he said the important words again, with more feeling than the first time. "I love you, Mary. You're the only woman for me."

That did it. Her heart melted.

When he reeled her in, she went. He cradled her close. They shared a long, sweet kiss. And then he carried her to her bedroom and made beautiful love to her.

Everything was good between them.

Except, well, it wasn't. Not in the way Mary had dreamed it might be.

As more weeks went by and May faded into June, she started to realize that they weren't really *together,* not in the deepest sense. He had his life and she had hers. He came to her in her life and seemed to really like being there, as she loved having him. But other than the occasional fancy meal in an expensive restaurant, she didn't go into his world.

She began to think that he wanted to keep her separate. He showered her in diamonds, bought out expensive baby boutiques for her child, paid the wages of her ranch hands.

But when it came down to it, she wasn't part of his real, everyday life. He'd yet to invite her to meet his parents or his brothers and sisters, though he'd been sleeping in her bed for over a month.

Yes, he had told her he loved her. And meant it. She really did believe that he meant it.

Now, though, she began to see that it wasn't just the words she wanted. As the days grew longer and hotter, she realized that what she wanted from Gabe Bravo was not only more than words, it was more than all the terrific things he'd done to make her life better, more than diamonds or fancy baby toys.

She wanted it all. She wanted her house to be his house. She wanted his ring on her finger. She wanted a life with him. A *real* life, not a fantasy.

She wanted to be Gabe's wife.

And since he wasn't leading the way on this issue, she was going to have to gut it up and tell the man what she wanted, just as she had made herself say *I love you* first.

The night she finally made the decision, it was the first Monday in June and he was out of town on a business trip.

But he would be back on Thursday. He'd already promised he would see her Thursday night.

So, all right. When he showed up Thursday, she would ask him to marry her.

Chapter Fourteen

Gabe and Davis got off the BravoCorp jet at a little after five Thursday afternoon. It had been a long trip from Madrid. BravoCorp was considering getting into the wine import business—Spanish wine, to start. Davis had wanted a Bravo-Corp attorney with him to take on any potential legal issues when he met with the prospective distributors. And if given his choice of lawyers, Davis always picked Gabe.

A limo was waiting. The driver put their luggage in the trunk and they were on their way.

"Stop by the house," Davis suggested. "We'll have a drink. Dinner, too, if you're open. Your mother will be happy to see you."

"Thanks, Dad. Another time, maybe." He was anxious to see Mary.

After a moment, Davis asked carefully, "Going out to the Lazy H?"

"That's right."

"You've been going there a lot lately—and don't give me that look, okay? I'm not butting in. It's only that your mother and I have been wondering why you never bring her around."

"Is that an invitation, Dad?"

"That is exactly what it is. How about Saturday, at the ranch? Mary might enjoy a tour of Bravo Ridge. I'll get your mother on it. She'll round up the whole family."

Gabe knew Mary would love that. So why did he hesitate? "It's a big step, the whole meet-the-family thing."

"Is that a no?" his father asked.

"Of course it's not a no. Tell you what. Let me get back to you."

"It's a straight-up invitation, Gabe. No tricks. Since this seems to be developing into something serious, I'd like to get to know her, and your mother would, too."

"I believe you, Dad. Thanks. I'll let you know."

Gabe called Mary from the car as soon as the driver dropped his dad off.

She answered on the first ring. "Gabe?"

Just the sound of her voice made him smile. "I'm on my way. About six-thirty?"

"I can't wait to see you." She sounded a little tense.

He almost asked her if there was a problem. But he'd be seeing her in less than an hour. If something was up, they could deal with it then. He said, "Be there soon," and hung up.

He thought about his father's invitation as he showered at his place, and shaved and dressed in jeans, comfortable boots and a T-shirt. He considered it some more as he drove to Mary's.

By the time he was getting out of the car in front of her house, he'd pretty much decided to turn his dad down. Maybe later.

For now, though, why complicate a really good thing? He couldn't imagine his life without Mary—and Ginny, too. He *loved* Mary, which was scary enough for now. Mary was like no other woman he had ever known. Smart and independent. And amazing in bed.

More amazing than he'd expected, if the truth were known. For a woman who had been flat-out terrified the first time they made love, she'd seriously gotten beyond her fear. It was one of the reasons—besides her humor and her intelligence and her decency as a human being—that he was hot-footing it to her place, jet lag be damned.

He couldn't wait to be with her, to kiss her, to touch her...

But as far as taking her to meet the family? Uh-uh. They didn't need to rush things. He liked his relationship with her just the way it was.

He stood for a minute when he got out of the car, a bouquet of flowers in one hand and a gift in the other, admiring the new paint job on the house. It looked good.

It would look even better if Mary would let him have the hands put on a new roof. And inside, the place could use a major makeover. He was even thinking he might try talking her into an add-on. A top-of-the-line kitchen, for certain. New furniture. The works.

He figured that eventually he would wear her down the way he did with most things. She would allow him to give her the house she deserved.

And where the hell was she? He'd been gone for five days. Usually after he'd been away, she would come flying out the front door to greet him.

With a shrug, he headed for the steps.

She opened the door just as he reached it. He smelled dinner. Something spicy. He couldn't wait. Mary was an excellent cook. She cooked almost as well as she made love.

"Hey," she said softly. One look in her eyes and he knew something wasn't right. She was anxious. And she'd set her chin at a determined angle.

It was the same expression she'd worn that night she told him she loved him. Then, it had scared him.

It scared him now, too. But in a completely different way, since he recognized that look now. He would have laid serious odds that a conversation about their relationship was in the offing. It was the last thing a guy needed after twelve hours on a plane.

Mary saw he had brought her flowers, which was sweet of him. And also something in a small, beautifully wrapped box. Probably jewelry. Which she'd told him to stop giving her.

The sight of the small box with its satin bow completely annoyed her. It made her stiffen her spine, made her all the more determined to have a little talk with him—now. Before she kissed him. Before he held Ginny.

Before she dragged him to the bedroom and ripped all his clothes off.

It was only going to get harder every time she put it off. And Mary Hofstetter was not the kind to procrastinate. Once she faced the fact that a thing needed doing, she waded right in.

He handed her the flowers.

"Thank you," she said. "We have to talk."

We have to talk? Where had that come from? Really, she

should have prepared a good opening line. This was going to be a marriage proposal, after all. No *guy* asked a woman to marry him by starting out with *We have to talk*.

She wanted to stop it, then. She wanted a do-over at some later date, when she was better prepared to start out a little smoother.

But seeing the wariness in his beautiful eyes, she was suddenly certain that it wouldn't have mattered how smooth she was. He simply didn't want to hear it.

He proved her right a second later. "Mary. Come on, I just got off a plane."

That got her back up. "Yes, well. I just spent all day in front of a computer. Except for the times I walked the floor with Ginny, who has been colicky—and I cooked breakfast, lunch and dinner. And cleaned up Brownie's vomit." In the corner, the dog gave a sheepish whine at the sound of her name. And well she should. She'd dragged a jumbo bag of Cheetos out of a drawer and eaten the whole thing, bag and all. The bag, apparently, hadn't agreed with her.

And Gabe was no fool. He got the message that the *Poor me, I've spent hours on a private jet* routine wasn't cutting it. He set the present with its perfect satin bow on a side table. "Is Ginny okay?"

"She's fine. It was colic, that's all."

He started toward the stairs. "Is she in her room?"

She sidestepped and blocked his path. "Gabe."

He blew out a breath. "Damn it, Mary. What's the problem?"

They had never had a fight, she realized at that moment. Because he really was a terrific man, a man who loved her and treated her right.

And because she had never pushed him about anything—

beyond getting him to say he loved her and asking him, please, not to bring her any more expensive jewelry.

No, they had never had a fight. But she had a really bad feeling they were about to have one now. "We do have to talk about this."

"This?"

"Yes. This. Us."

"No." He spoke softly. Almost hopefully. "We don't. We don't *have* to talk about it. You could just let it go."

She did consider that, letting it go. Again. Seriously. Maybe he had it right. Now wasn't a good time. She should choose a better one.

But *when* was a better time? There was no better time when the man you loved simply didn't want to hear it.

"Gabe, I…there are things that are bothering me, about us. About where we're going, which is basically nowhere."

He turned and strode toward the kitchen, stopping in the arch that divided it from the living area. For a moment, he just stood there, his back to her. With effort, she kept her mouth shut and waited for him to face her again.

Finally, he did. "Is there some reason we have to *go* somewhere? What's wrong with where we are? I thought you were happy."

Gently, she laid the bouquet on the coffee table, bending and straightening with slow care. "I am happy. But I'm not…*happy*."

He raked a hand back through his hair. "I don't know what the hell you're talking about."

"Oh, Gabe. I think you do." He was so far away. He should be closer. It should all be different. Better. More romantic and tender. But it wasn't. It was…what it was. And she needed to stop lying to herself about it. She needed to tell the truth. "Gabe, I feel like I'm your mistress or something."

He made a low noise of disbelief at that, and shook his head in a disgusted way.

"Wait," she said. "Hear me out. I mean, I *am* your mistress, really, aren't I? Or whatever they call it nowadays. You keep me tucked away. I never go into your world, you come to mine. And you *buy* me. You shower me with expensive gifts, you spend thousands on fixing up my ranch. You *hire* people to work for me."

His blue eyes flashed with hurt anger. "What? Now you resent that I helped you out a little."

"No. Absolutely not. I don't resent you or any of the great things you've done for me. Not in any way. Except for the jewelry you won't stop giving me, I appreciate everything, all of it. You've been so good to me and I know it. But the problem is, Gabe. I'm really not the mistress type."

The anger had faded from his eyes. He came toward her, at last, and reached for her hand. Hope rose, warm and sweet, within her as his fingers closed around hers.

"Mary..." He said the word so tenderly. Maybe she really was getting through to him. "Come on." He led her to the sofa. They sat down. She almost believed it would be all right.

Then he asked, "What's happened? Has someone been giving you heartache about you and me? Just tell me. I'll handle it."

She let out a soft cry of disappointment and frustration. So much for daring to imagine she might be getting through to him. "I do not believe you just said that."

"Answer my question. Who is it?"

"Handle it?" She pulled her hand free of his. "You'll *handle* it? Oh. Because you're the fixer, right? I tell you who's been saying mean things about me and you go 'fix' them?"

"Who *is* it?" he demanded, stubborn as a slab of stone. He wasn't getting it. He *refused* to get it.

"Let me be more direct," she said through clenched teeth.

"I wish to hell you would."

"There's no one. Honestly. No one but you. And me. It's us, Gabe. *We're* giving me heartache."

"Okay." He put up both hands as if she had a gun on him. "I give. What, exactly, is it you want from me?"

It was the pertinent question. The urge rose again, to evade. To put it off. But he had asked. Finally. At last.

So she answered. "I want to be part of your world, Gabe. I want to meet your family. And I want to marry you. I'm in no big rush about it. It doesn't have to be today. Or next week or next month. But someday in the not-*too*-distant future, please. I love you with all my heart and I want us to be a family—you and me and Ginny and any other babies we might be fortunate enough to have. That's what I want. Marriage. And a life with you, a life at your side, not *on* the side."

He stared at her as if she'd just hit him over the head with a large, blunt object. "Married," he said bleakly. "You want to get married…."

She refused to even flinch. "Yes, I do. What about you?"

He rose. And he started walking. In the center of the room, he stopped and turned to her. For several endless seconds he just stared at her. And then he shrugged. "Fine," he said flatly. "All right. If that's what you need to be happy, we'll get married."

Mary let out a cry of pure distress. She started to rise. But when he backed up a step, making it clear he didn't want her near him right then, she sank to the cushions again. "Oh, Gabe, no. Don't…say you'll marry me just because *I* want it. That's not what I want. That could never work."

He shook his head. "Hold on. Just hold the hell on. Let me get clear on this. You not only want me to marry you, to promise we'll be together till we're both old and gray, you want me to convince you that what you want is what *I* want. Well, I don't. I just want *you,* Mary. I always have, since the day you almost had Ginny in the backseat of my Escalade. I want you. That's the bottom line. And whatever I have to do to keep you, I'll do it."

"Gabe," she pleaded. "Will you listen to yourself? You grew up with married parents—two people who love each other and are happy in their marriage. I can't believe you think we can be happy together if you don't even want to be married to me."

"Happy." His lip curled in a sneer. "Come on. You've laid down your terms and I've accepted them. I'll marry you whenever and wherever you say. It's settled. Oh, and my father invited you out to Bravo Ridge for a family get-together this weekend. So there you have it. You'll be meeting the family. That should satisfy your other demand."

"Demand?" How had this gotten so far out of hand? "That's not right, and you know it. I never made any demands."

"Sure as hell sounded like you did to me."

Should she have known that bringing up marriage to him would be like waving a red flag in front of a big, mad bull? She just hadn't. Yes, she'd been ready for his reluctance and his attempts at avoidance. She'd even been prepared for a sweet and smoothly done refusal.

But not this…raging acceptance. It wasn't like him, not like him at all. Somehow, she'd managed to hit a major nerve with him.

"Gabe." She stood, slowly, as if he were some wild creature she'd let in the house, one that might attack if she made any sudden moves. He watched her, every muscle in his big body drawn tight, as she approached. She stopped maybe four feet away from him, not daring to move closer, and she pleaded with outstretched arms. "Gabe, please. I…" She had no idea how to go on. She let her arms drop and she stared at him, feeling hopeless, just completely out of her depth.

Somehow, her half-finished plea and the painful silence that followed reached him when all her passionate arguments had only fanned the fire. His body relaxed, his wide shoulders slumping.

And she cleared the final distance between them. She looked up into his eyes, seeking…something. Reassurance, maybe. A few words to let her know his irrational anger had left him.

He gave her those words. "I'm sorry." He rubbed his eyes, like a man waking from a trance. "That was way out of line. I just…I lost it." He shook his head, bewildered. "I never lose it…"

Ginny chose that moment to wake up and start fussing. They both heard her cries from the baby monitor on the kitchen table. Mary knew a sweet relief at the sudden excuse to do something other than stand there and stare at him, to try and start picking up the pieces after the cruel things he had said.

Gabe seemed relieved, too. "Let's go see what she wants."

So they went up and took care of the baby. When she

was fed and changed, Gabe carried her downstairs and sat with her on the sofa while Mary got the dinner on the table.

She called him to eat. He put the baby down on the play mat he'd bought her and Ginny lay there, making happy little noises, staring up at the brightly colored mobile that had come with the mat.

The meal was a silent one, painfully so. Later, he carried Ginny back up to bed. When he came down, he took Mary's hand and led her to the bedroom.

They undressed in silence. In bed, he kissed her. But that was all. She turned in his arms and he held her, loosely. It didn't feel right to make love that night. There was a scary distance between them now. She didn't know how to bridge it.

Apparently, neither did he.

In the morning, when she woke to a sliver of sunlight peeking between the curtains, he was already awake, lying on his side, watching her.

He touched her night-tangled hair, smoothing it. And he spoke to her, softly. "When I was a kid, my parents had some kind of almost-breakup. They fought all the time, slept in separate rooms for a while. My dad even moved out for a couple of weeks. To me, well, it just felt like the collapse of my world was coming. That nothing would be right again, you know?"

She nodded, and she freed a hand from under the sheet to brush the back of it along his beard-rough cheek.

"I don't think the littler kids had any idea what was going on, but Ash and I were the oldest. Old enough to know there was a problem. A big one. Old enough to know what divorce was, and to be certain it was happening in our family."

"But they didn't divorce. They got through it. And now they have a good marriage…"

"That's right. They did get past it. And they're happy now, together. Ash used to tell me they would work it out. He would play the big brother so well, tell me not to sweat it. There was no way *our* mom and dad would get a divorce. It turned out he was right. They worked it out, whatever it was. But in the meantime, while they battled, I remember thinking it just wasn't worth it, that I would never get married. I would be single and happy. And I have been."

"Until I came along and…messed with the program?"

He made a sound that might have been a laugh. Or a groan. "That's about the size of it."

They were silent for a time, just lying there in the early morning quiet.

Then he said what he'd said last night, only this time he spoke tenderly. "I do love you, Mary. I want you to have what you want. And if it's marriage, you got it."

Oh, she longed to wrap her arms around him and whisper her *yes* against his warm lips, to tell herself that love would conquer all in the end, that in time he would be glad she had forced his hand. But the truth remained. "It's not what *you* want, though, is it?"

"What can I say?"

"How about yes or no?"

It took him a minute. But then, he admitted, "Uh-uh. Marriage isn't what I want."

She nodded. Yeah, it hurt to hear it. But the truth was like that sometimes.

He said, "And I take it you don't feel right about going on as we have been."

She looked in his eyes. "No, Gabe. I don't."

"So I guess that means we're in for a little time apart."

She touched him again, laying her hand against his throat, loving the feel of him, wondering how she would bear the days—and the nights—without him. Tenderness welled up within her. He had put it so kindly, *a little time apart.* But they both knew he meant that this was it. They were breaking up.

He pressed his forehead to hers. And he sighed. And against her thigh, she felt him, soft and smooth. Limp. Vulnerable.

She reached down and touched him, cradling him. He sucked in a hard breath, responding instantly to her caress.

"Mary." He said her name on a rough husk of breath. "Are you sure?"

She stroked him, nodding. It seemed to her the best way, the most beautiful way, to say goodbye. "One last time…"

With a groan, he reached for her. Eight weeks had passed since they first made love, eight weeks since she'd started on the pill. They no longer had to bother with condoms. She took him in her arms, pulling him down on top of her, opening her legs for him.

But it was no good. She wasn't ready. He felt her body's resistance and he lifted away to look down at her again. He smiled at her.

And she smiled back, a wobbly, sad little smile. "I love you."

"And I love you." He touched her, then, gently. Teasingly, at first. His knowing fingers played her so well. He knew what aroused her, what made her body open like a flower in the sun.

It didn't take long and she was moaning, moving her hips against his stroking hand, urging him to come to her, to fill her, one more time.

And he did. He eased her thighs apart and settled between them again. That time, when he pushed in, her body gave no resistance.

With a low moan of pure pleasure, she accepted him. She wrapped her arms and legs around him and they began to move. Together, as one.

It lasted for a long time. It was the sweetest small eternity.

In the end, he rolled them, so she could take the top position. She rose up, pressing down at the same time, claiming him even more fully than before.

He took her hips in his two hands and surged up inside her as she met his thrusts, bending her body close to him, kissing his neck, his shoulders, pressing her lips right over his heart as she rode him. When he came, he pushed himself up to her and then held still as he spilled himself inside her. She watched his face, memorizing it, for all the days to come.

"I love you, Gabe Bravo." And her climax took her, filling her up, spilling over until every nerve in her body sang of sweet fulfillment.

Afterward, they had no time to laze around, to draw out their goodbye.

The baby cried. And the hands needed breakfast.

Later, she walked him out to his Escalade for the last time. The sun was a third of the way up in the sky by then and white, cottony clouds floated so prettily up there in the blue.

He told her, "I'm going to go on paying wages for Wyatt and Ty. Don't argue with me, okay? We've been through this. They need the jobs and you need the help. I've also put them on health insurance plans. You and Ginny, too." When she opened her mouth to protest that it was way too much, he put a finger against her lips. "Shh. It's no biggie for me. And it will make me feel good, to know I don't have to worry that you have what you need."

She swallowed down her protests and nodded. It was the best she could manage at that moment. The hard tumble of a hundred emotions had stolen her voice.

He continued. "I'll have all the paperwork sent to you, so you'll be in control."

She managed a shaky, "Okay."

"And there's a college trust fund for Ginny. I'll send you the papers on that, too."

Mary sucked in a sharp breath and put her hand over her mouth. Again she nodded. And somehow she got three words out. "Thank you, Gabe."

He lifted her chin with a finger. "Take care of yourself, Mary."

"You, too."

"And Ginny…"

"I will."

And then he got in the Escalade. She stepped back as he started the car up and put it in gear. And then she made herself stand there, watching, arms wrapped tight around her middle, as he left her for the last time.

She refused to let a single tear fall until he was out of sight.

Chapter Fifteen

Inside, she found that the flowers he'd brought her the night before were too wilted to save. And the present still waited on the side table, behind the lamp, where he'd set it. She tossed the flowers. It would have hurt too much to have to look at them, anyway.

She dithered over the gift, knowing how he was. She would only insult him if she sent it back. Still, she wasn't willing to open it and keep it for herself. In the end, she took it, fancy wrapping and all, and put it in the top of her closet, in the back. Maybe someday she would give it to Ginny, tell her it was from a man who had once loved both of them very much.

After that, well, she had articles due, a baby to raise and a ranch to take care of. In the days that followed, as June became July and summer brought temperatures in the triple-digits two weeks in a row, she missed Gabe. So much.

His absence was like an empty ache in the center of her. When it got too bad, she would hold Ginny close, breathe in the sweet baby smell of her skin, and tell herself the hurt would pass. Her love would fade. Or if it didn't, it would change. Become something gentler, easier to bear.

Sometimes, alone in bed at night, she talked to Rowdy. She told him how certain she was that she had done the right thing, sending Gabe away. But oh, it did hurt. It made her heart feel like a tattered thing, forlorn and dragging, inside her chest.

Rowdy never answered when she talked to him. Dead men rarely do. But thinking of him, imagining the encouraging things he might have said, well, it did make her feel better. It made her stronger, kind of put things in perspective for her. A person made the best choices she could.

And life went on.

Ida knew she was hurting. After Mary told her mother-in-law that Gabe was gone and wouldn't be back, Ida made a point to come out to the house every other day, at least. And though she was not a very physical woman, except with her granddaughter, she would hug Mary more. She would reach across the table and touch Mary's hand. And Mary would think how fortunate she was. To have a friend like Ida, a baby like Ginny, work she loved and a fine place to call home.

Her friends dropped by often. Garland came and helped out Ty and Wyatt with a few things around the ranch and then stayed for whatever meal was available. Donna Lynn showed up once a week, at least. And so did Mary's other friends from town.

On the Fourth of July, the chamber of commerce in Wulf City threw a big picnic in Wulf Park. Mary took

Ginny and joined Ida, Donna Lynn and most of Donna Lynn's family. They played softball and roasted hot dogs. And when dark came, there were fireworks. Mary watched the bright explosions in the Texas sky and wondered if Gabe was watching fireworks somewhere, too.

Four times during those first tough weeks after Gabe left her, tired-looking men in worn jeans and broken-down boots came to her door in need of somewhere to lay their heads for the night. As always, she fed them and let them sleep in the barn. And she smiled to herself, thinking how, if Gabe were there, he would probably have hired each and every one of them. She would be the only woman in Texas with a hundred and twenty acres, a few bad-tempered goats and six ranch hands.

But Gabe wasn't there. And she was getting used to that, making her peace with it. She was. She truly was....

After he left Mary, Gabe worked. A lot. Any project, any time. That was pretty much his motto.

His dad had found out right away that he and Mary were through. Gabe told him flat out that it was over when Davis asked if he would be bringing Mary to the ranch on the weekend. Davis said he was sorry it hadn't worked out. He actually sounded sincere. Gabe thanked him and left it at that. His father had been as good as his word about leaving Mary alone. BravoCorp had bought another ranch not far from Mary's. The Bravo River project was well underway.

Two weeks later, his mother dropped by the office. She tried to get him to "open up" about how he was doing. When that went nowhere, she gently asked if maybe he would like to go out with another of the daughters of a friend of hers, a sweet Texas debutante named Bunny McDuke.

Gabe decided he needed to quit moping around. One of his mother's "nice girls" would be about right, for now. He wasn't up for having sex yet and a girl like Bunny McDuke wouldn't be wanting to have sex with him, anyway. Not on the first date.

Bunny was small and blond and bouncy. She laughed a lot. Gabe took her out to the country club he and everyone in his family had belonged to all his life. They had dinner in the clubhouse. And then they went dancing. Bunny got up good and close during the slow numbers. She laughed and rubbed her plump breasts against him.

When he took her home, she grabbed him around the neck and stuck her tongue down his throat. He gently peeled her off him and told her good-night.

On the drive home, he almost took the turn that would get him to the Lazy H. But he held the wheel steady and drove on home.

A couple more weeks went by. He worked late. He left town on two three-day business trips. He went out with friends now and then, in groups. Groups, he decided, were the way to go. For now. Groups or parties, where he could arrive on his own and leave when he felt like it.

He got offers—from women he met at those parties, from an old girlfriend in town for the night. And he knew he had his reputation as the Bravo Bachelor to uphold. But so what? He just wasn't in the mood.

Not yet. He was giving it time, he told himself. He was in love—scratch that. He *had been* in love for the first time in his life. He had a right to take a few weeks to get over it.

Too bad, as more days and weeks went by without Mary—and without Ginny—he only felt more miserable. And lonely as hell. He could almost wish he'd never met her.

Except he couldn't imagine not having met Mary, not having held Ginny in his arms. He missed them. Bad.

So bad he was even starting to get a glimmer of what a thick-headed idiot he'd been.

By the second Friday in July, six weeks and a day after she and Gabe ended it, Mary was starting to feel that she was pulling it together. Every day, hours would go by when she didn't even think of Gabe. Her heart, she kept telling herself, had started to heal.

Still, nights were tough. By then, Ginny was sleeping straight through from about ten to six. Mary had all those hours of darkness to herself. Too much time to brood, really. So she had been taking on extra assignments from the various editors she wrote for and she would often work until midnight, concentrating on getting words on the screen, keeping her mind from wandering places there was no reason to go.

That night she was at her computer around seven when someone knocked on the door. She answered to find another down-on-his-luck drifter. This one had a handsome face lined early by hardship and too much time in the sun. A grimy-looking bedroll and a backpack waited at his feet and he held the stub of a cigarette between his lips. Before saying a word, he crushed what was left of the cigarette under his worn boot and stuck the butt in the breast pocket of his battered denim jacket.

Then he swiped off his straw cowboy hat. "Ma'am, I heard tell you don't mind if a man sleeps in your barn for a night."

She tried not to think of Gabe, not to wonder if he would have insisted on hiring this guy, too. "Of course I don't mind." At her request, Ty and Wyatt had spent a day closing off a corner of the barn, making a small, private area for any wanderer who needed a place to lay his head.

"There's a door to the right as you enter the barn," she told him. "You can sleep in there." The room held a bed and an old night table. Ty and Wyatt had run a line in there for light. "Are you hungry?"

"I could use a little something, if it won't put you out."

She made him two sandwiches and added an apple and a square of spice cake Ida had brought by the day before. He was painfully polite. "Thank you so much, ma'am. For everything."

"My pleasure. Sleep well."

"I will, ma'am. Thanks to you."

She nodded and shut the door, smiling a little at the way the guy had called her "ma'am," just like Rowdy always used to do. And then she went back to her computer and worked for another few hours on a quilting piece for *Country Ways Monthly.*

Later, after she'd fed and diapered Ginny and put her in her crib for the night, she had a long, slow soak in the tub and then climbed into bed.

There was a full moon out, hovering huge and silvery above the barn. So she left the curtains open and stared at it for a long time, thinking how cool and distant it looked—and longing for Gabe.

The truth kind of snuck up on her, as she lay there, unable to sleep.

She had to admit it: Her love wasn't fading. She wasn't getting over him, she was…denying him. Denying the love she felt for him. Trying to bury it, to call it gone, to say she had healed. As if her love was no more than a messy wound she could stitch up and slap a bandage on. And then wait for it to fade to a thin, white scar.

As she stared at the faraway face of the man in the moon, she started seeing her own stubbornness. Her blindness. She started thinking the impossible, thinking that maybe it *wasn't* impossible. Not impossible at all—to let loving him be enough. To let what they had just *be,* to stop demanding more of him than he was willing, freely, to give.

Okay, he had some hang-up about marriage. But he did love her. He'd said it. And more important, he'd shown it in a thousand ways. He'd been so good to her, always doing whatever he could, going the extra mile for her. Even when he'd left her, he'd gone with her child's education paid for, her ranch spiffed up, all the dangerous dead brush cleared away, with Ty and Wyatt to help her—and insurance for all of them.

He might not be a man who would ever marry her. But so what? He gave her so much. Why couldn't she let that be enough?

She *could,* she was starting to realize. She wanted commitment from him and he'd already given her that. She could loosen up a little. She could be the one to compromise.

Mary threw back the covers and padded on bare feet to the closet. She slid the door wide and got way in the back and stood on tiptoe to get the last gift he had brought her. And then she sat on the bed and opened it by the light of the moon, sighing in pleasure when she lifted it from its velvet box.

A bracelet—alternating diamonds and sapphires—to match the necklace he had given her before. She put it on. And then she got back under the covers.

She missed him. So very much. She could see the light in the barn, a glow from the small window in the makeshift bedroom where another man without much to call his own had bedded down for the night. She lay snug in her own house on the land she loved, but she felt lonely. Maybe lonelier than that guy in the barn.

Tomorrow, she thought.

Tomorrow she would go to Gabe. She would ask to try again. Maybe he would turn her down. He could very likely have moved beyond her by now. He could say he was doing fine and didn't want to get involved with her again.

If he refused her love, so be it. She would never know if she didn't try.

Mary let her eyes drift shut. She felt relaxed and easy in her skin for the first time in six weeks. The decision was made and with it came a certain peace. Sleep closed over her, sweet and deep.

She woke suddenly, bolting upright.

Someone was pounding on the back door, calling her name. "Mary! Mary, wake up!"

Blinking in sleepy surprise, she glanced toward the window. It was still night out there and the moon had gone down.

But it wasn't the darkness that had her crying out in distress.

The barn was on fire.

She threw on a robe and raced to the door.

Wyatt, bare-chested in a pair of old Wranglers, with a serious case of bedhead, said, "Get the baby and come outside. The wind's blowing toward the house."

"The fire department…"

"I've already called them. Just get the baby and get outside."

"Yes. All right. I will…."

Wyatt didn't hang around to see if she was doing what he'd told her to do. He ran toward the barn where Ty already had a hose turned on full blast, trying to keep the blaze under control until the county's volunteer firefighters arrived.

Her pulse echoing in her ears, Mary hustled upstairs barefooted to get Ginny. She scooped the sleeping darling up in her arms and swung the diaper bag onto a shoulder.

Back downstairs, she set Ginny on the bed while she tugged on a pair of boots. Then she picked up the baby, grabbed her purse and settled it and the diaper bag over her spare shoulder. What else? Her work.

She hurried to the living room to get the memory stick with her recent projects on it. The stick hung from a lanyard on a pin by the computer. She lifted it free and slipped it over her head.

And then she fled through the back door, only pausing to call Brownie, who came running at the sound of her name. Outside, the flames were brighter than before. Ginny's stroller waited beneath the patio cover. Mary tucked her in there, nice and safe.

"Stay, Brownie." The dog dropped to her haunches. Mary left her there with Ginny and went to see if she could help. The patio cover, she figured, would protect the baby from any random sparks.

Ty still had the hose on the blaze. Wyatt had dragged the other hose around from the front. He was wetting the roof of the house, trying to douse the flying sparks before they could catch the old, dry roof shingles on fire.

"The baby?" he shouted at her.

"On the back patio," she told him.

"Better stick with her. This thing could get loose and take the house any time now."

She feared he was right. And there wasn't a lot she could do, anyway. She might have manned a hose herself. There were other faucets on the property—at the horse trough and in the goat yard. Too bad the extra hoses were in the barn and there was no going near it by now.

The flames had eaten their way along the walls and up over the roof, turning the dry old walls and ancient roof shakes to an inferno. It would be burned to ash in no time…

Oh, God. That poor man she'd let sleep in the corner room! She sent a prayer winging heavenward that he wasn't in there, that somehow he'd managed to get out before the fire or the smoke overpowered him.

At least all the animals should be okay. By the blazing light the fire provided, she could see the two horses, milling around at the far side of their paddock. The goats had moved to the back of their yard, too. She could hear them out there, baaaaing like crazy, some of them even making outraged screeching sounds. But they were away from the building, safe outside.

The chicken coop was several hundred feet from the barn. But what if a random spark found it and it caught fire?

Mary glanced toward the patio. Brownie sat patiently next to the stroller. It should be safe for her to see to the chickens…

She ran, clutching her robe tight around her, the boots she'd pulled on rough against her heels—she hadn't wanted to waste the extra seconds finding socks. The coop was over by the cabin where Ty and Wyatt lived, off to itself. And the wind was blowing the other way.

Still, she could hear the chickens in there, agitated, fluttering around. She threw the coop door wide. The chickens fluttered and pecked each other, but they didn't emerge.

They weren't the brightest creatures in the animal kingdom. She had to go in there and chase them out.

Freed, they ran around the yard in circles, clucking and fluttering. Mary shooed them out of the way and ran to check on Ginny.

The barn roof came down just as she ducked beneath the shelter of the patio cover. It made a terrible whooshing sound and then collapsed in on itself, sparks shooting skyward, thousands of them, most of them blowing right for the house. Brownie whined in fear.

"Move away!" Ty shouted. "Get clear of the house, Mary!" By then he'd given up on dousing the barn and had turned his hose, with Wyatt's, on the roof of the house.

Mary hooked the diaper bag and her purse over her arm again, and flipped the shade of the stroller to cover the baby's head. Brownie at her heels, she rolled the stroller as fast as she could away from the fire and the house, toward Wyatt and Ty's cabin and the open chicken coop.

By then Ginny was wailing. Mary picked her up and rocked her from side to side, staring in disbelief at what was left of the barn.

Then, grimly, she turned her gaze to the house. She watched, helpless, as numberless embers gently drifted, glowing bright, onto the roof. Wyatt and Ty watered most of them to wet ash. But there were simply too many.

The section of roof over her bedroom caught all at once. One moment it was only an ember, red as a dragon's eye, and the next, with a wild rush of sound, a raging blaze. The water the two men aimed at it seemed to do no more than slow it down—for a few seconds. Then the flames rose up again, hungry. Roaring.

Mary stared, sick at heart, as her house burned.

And then, at last, the sounds of sirens filled the night. She saw the lights from around the front of the house. They were too late to save the barn. But maybe, if the good Lord, and a little luck, was with them, they would manage to save her home.

Once the firefighters took over, Mary called Ida. Her mother-in-law arrived in fifteen minutes flat.

Then she and Ida stood side-by-side, Ida holding the baby, out of the way, as the firefighters did what they could. It didn't take long after that. Within minutes of Ida's arrival, the fire was out.

The barn and the master bedroom were smoldering piles of wet ash, though the rest of the house still stood. The fire marshal arrived with a clipboard and a whole bunch of questions. He shooed a couple of chickens out of his way and took Wyatt aside first.

"It could have been worse," Ida said softly.

Mary nodded. "I think it started in the corner of the barn where I had Ty and Wyatt build that sleeping alcove. When Wyatt woke me up, I looked out the window and saw that corner of the barn on fire."

Ida sent her a look. "Someone staying in there?"

"Yeah." Mary spoke softly.

"No sign of him since the fire started?"

"Nope."

Ty, shooing chickens back toward the coop, heard them talking. He stopped with a fat white hen tucked under his arm. "The guy in the barn, you mean? He ran away— though he did stop to knock on the cabin door and warn us first. When Wyatt answered, he pointed at the barn, yelled, 'fire,' and then took off running." The chicken clucked and he stroked its white feathers. "You'd think he might have had the guts to stick around and give us a hand."

Mary shook her head. "He was probably scared to death he would be blamed."

Ty grunted. "The fire started in the part of the barn where he was staying. And it doesn't take much. Probably dropped off to sleep with a lit cigarette in his mouth. So his being scared he'd take blame? That ain't no excuse, not where I come from." He left them to gather up the rest of the chickens.

"Well." Ida tucked the baby blanket closer around Ginny. "At least we know he got away."

Mary agreed. "It's so good to know he's all right. I've been dreading the worst, worrying over what might have happened…."

Ida shifted the baby to one arm and wrapped the other around Mary's shoulders. Mary sagged against her, thankful that no one had been hurt after all, and glad for Ida's steady presence at her side.

Beyond the smoking roof of the house, dawn was breaking. A rooster, perched on the fence of the goat yard, let out his morning cry.

And it was then, as Mary leaned on Ida and the sun came up, that the black Escalade came flying around from the front of the house, dodging the fire trucks and the firefighters' equipment, only slowing when the driver had a clear view of Mary and Ida, with Brownie at their feet and Ginny held safe in Ida's arms.

Chapter Sixteen

Her heart soaring, tears blurring her eyes, Mary glanced at Ida.

Her mother-in-law shrugged. "He stopped in the hardware store after you two broke up, gave me a bunch of phone numbers, told me to call him right away if you ever needed him. I figured he'd probably want to know your ranch was on fire."

"Oh, Ida…"

"You go on, now. He'll be wanting to see for himself, up close, that you're all right. Brownie." She clucked her tongue at the dog, who was already up on all fours and wagging her tail. "Stay."

Mary turned as Gabe emerged from that shiny black car. Had there ever in this world been a man so handsome and proud?

She ran to him. And he opened his arms to her and

gathered her in, whispering her name against her hair. "Mary. Mary…"

She looked up into his face and she saw the love there and she knew then that whatever happened from that moment on, they would be getting through it together.

He took her face in his two hands. "No more of this." His voice was rough with barely contained emotion. "I can't stand it. *You're* what I want, you and Ginny. You are my love. My only love. Whatever you want, Mary. However you want it. I'll marry you in a minute. I swear it. I'm here now, and I've got you in my arms. And I am never letting go." He kissed her then, her lips, her cheeks, her nose, her chin—a rain of kisses, falling fast and sweet.

"Gabe. Oh, Gabe…." She lifted up on tiptoe and pressed her mouth to his in a kiss that was long and deep. And when she finally dropped back on her heels, she told him, "I love you. I should have been more patient, more understanding." She touched the side of his face, in wonderment that he was really there, with her, again. At last.

He caught her wrist, and smiled in pleasure to see she wore the bracelet he'd bought for her.

She sniffed back joyful tears. "I'm so glad I finally had the sense to open that pretty box you left behind. The other beautiful things you gave me…they were in the jewelry box in my bedroom, and my bedroom is gone."

He looked at her with the same joy she knew was shining in her own eyes. "They're only things, Mary. You and Ginny are safe. Everyone came out alive, right?" He waited for her nod before he added, "That's what matters."

She whispered, "I was coming to get you, Gabe. Today, as a matter of fact. But here you are. Oh, Gabe. Here you are…"

"I love you, Mary." He said it softly, honestly, with no hesitation, looking straight in her eyes. "Marry me. Please."

"Oh, Gabe. Are you sure?"

"I wouldn't be asking you if I wasn't." He took her by the shoulders, his gaze steady. True. "Believe me, it's not a thing I take lightly."

"Then, yes. Oh, yes!" She grabbed him close again.

They held each other there in the dusty yard, the smell of soggy ash heavy in the air, by the smoldering ruin that had been the barn, oblivious to the firefighters rolling their hoses, stowing their ladders, getting ready to go.

The sky grew lighter. Morning had come.

And the Bravo Bachelor had found his own true love, at last.

* * * * *

*Celebrate 60 years of pure reading
pleasure with Harlequin®!*

*Step back in time and enjoy a sneak preview of an
exciting anthology from Harlequin® Historical with
THE DIAMONDS OF WELBOURNE MANOR*

This compelling anthology features three stories about
the outrageous Fitzmanning sisters. Meet Annalise,
who is never at a loss for words… But that can change
with an unexpected encounter in the forest.

Available May 2009 from Harlequin® Historical.

"I'm the illegitimate daughter of notoriously scandalous parents, Mr. Milford. Candidates for my hand are unlikely to be lining up at the gates."

"Don't be so quick to discount your charms, my dear. Or the charm of your substantial dowry. Or even your brothers' influence. There are as many reasons to marry as there are marriages."

Annalise snorted. "Oh, yes. Perhaps I shall marry for dynastic reasons, or perhaps for property or influence. After all, a loveless, practical marriage worked out so well for my mother."

"Well, you've routed me on that one. I can think of no suitable rejoinder." Ned rose to his feet and extended his hand. "And since that is the case, let me be the first to wish you a long and happy spinsterhood."

Her mouth gaped open. And then she laughed.

And he froze.

This was the first time, Ned realized. The first time he'd seen her eyes light up and her mouth curl. The first time he'd witnessed her features melded together in glorious accord to produce exquisite beauty.

Unbelievable what a change came over her face. Unheard of what effect her throaty, rasping laughter had on his body. It pounded a beat upon his ear, quickly taken up by his pulse. It echoed through him, finally residing in his stirring nether regions.

So easily she did it, awakened these sensations within him—without any apparent effort at all. And she had called him potentially dangerous? Clearly the intelligent thing for him to do would be to steer clear, to leave her to the tender ministrations of Lord Peter Blackthorne.

"You were right." She smiled up at him as she took his hand and climbed to her feet. "I do feel better."

Ah, well. When had he ever chosen the intelligent path?

He did not relinquish her hand. He used it to pull her in, close enough that he could feel the warmth of her. "At the risk of repeating Lord Peter's mistake and anticipating too much—may I ask if you'll be my partner in battledore tomorrow?"

Her smiled dimmed. Her breath came a little faster. His own had gone shallow, as if he'd just run a race—and lost. He ran his gaze over the appealing lift of her brow and the curious angle of her chin. His index finger twitched.

"I should like that," she said.

His finger trembled again and he lifted it, traced the pink and tender shell of her ear, the unique sweep of her jaw. Her pulse leaped beneath her skin, triggering his own. Slowly he tilted her chin up, waiting for her to object, to step back, to slap his hand away.

She did none of those eminently sensible things. Which left him free to do the entirely impractical thing.

Baby soft, the skin of her lips. Her whole body trembled when he touched her there.

He leaned in. Her eyes closed, even as she stood straight against him, strung as tight as a bow. He pressed his mouth to hers. It was a soft kiss, sweet and chaste. And yet he was hot and hard and as ready as he'd ever been in his life.

She drew back a little. Sighed. Their breath mingled a moment before she slowly backed away.

"Oh," she breathed. Her dark eyes were full of wonder and something that looked like fear. He took a step toward her, but she only shook her head. His outstretched hand fell to his side as she turned to disappear into the wood. This was the first time, Ned realized. The first time, since he'd come to the house party at Welbourne Manor, that he'd seen her eyes light up.

* * * * *

Follow Ned and Annalise's story in May 2009 in
THE DIAMONDS OF WELBOURNE MANOR
Available May 2009 from Harlequin® Historical

Available in the series romance section,
or in the historical romance section,
wherever books are sold.

**We'll be spotlighting a different series
every month throughout 2009
to celebrate our 60th anniversary.**

Look for Harlequin® Historical in May!

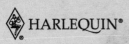

LAURA MARIE ALTOM
The Marine's Babies

Men Made in America

Captain Jace Monroe is everything a Marine should be—strong, brave and honorable. He's also an instant father of twin baby girls he never knew existed! Life gets even more complicated when he finds himself attracted to Emma Stewart, his new nanny. But can this sexy, fun-loving bachelor do the right thing and become a family man? Emma and the babies are counting on it!

**Available in May
wherever books are sold.**

LOVE, HOME & HAPPINESS

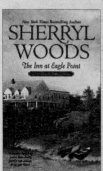
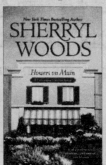
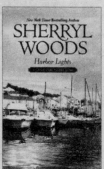

REQUEST YOUR FREE BOOKS!

2 FREE NOVELS PLUS 2 FREE GIFTS!

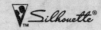

SPECIAL EDITION®

Life, Love and Family!

YES! Please send me 2 FREE Silhouette Special Edition® novels and my 2 FREE gifts (gifts are worth about $10). After receiving them, if I don't wish to receive any more books, I can return the shipping statement marked "cancel." If I don't cancel, I will receive 6 brand-new novels every month and be billed just $4.24 per book in the U.S. or $4.99 per book in Canada. That's a savings of at least 15% off the cover price! It's quite a bargain! Shipping and handling is just 25¢ per book*. I understand that accepting the 2 free books and gifts places me under no obligation to buy anything. I can always return a shipment and cancel at any time. Even if I never buy another book from Silhouette, the two free books and gifts are mine to keep forever.

235 SDN EEYU   335 SDN EEY6

Name	(PLEASE PRINT)	
Address		Apt. #
City	State/Prov.	Zip/Postal Code

Signature (if under 18, a parent or guardian must sign)

Mail to the **Silhouette Reader Service:**
IN U.S.A.: P.O. Box 1867, Buffalo, NY 14240-1867
IN CANADA: P.O. Box 609, Fort Erie, Ontario L2A 5X3

Not valid to current subscribers of Silhouette Special Edition books.

Want to try two free books from another line?
Call 1-800-873-8635 or visit www.morefreebooks.com.

* Terms and prices subject to change without notice. Prices do not include applicable taxes. Sales tax applicable in N.Y. Canadian residents will be charged applicable provincial taxes and GST. Offer not valid in Quebec. This offer is limited to one order per household. All orders subject to approval. Credit or debit balances in a customer's account(s) may be offset by any other outstanding balance owed by or to the customer. Please allow 4 to 6 weeks for delivery. Offer available while quantities last.

Your Privacy: Silhouette is committed to protecting your privacy. Our Privacy Policy is available online at www.eHarlequin.com or upon request from the Reader Service. From time to time we make our lists of customers available to reputable third parties who may have a product or service of interest to you. If you would prefer we not share your name and address, please check here. ☐

SSE09

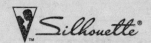
Silhouette®

COMING NEXT MONTH
Available April 28, 2009

SPECIAL EDITION

#1969 IN CARE OF SAM BEAUDRY—Kathleen Eagle
Maggie Whiteside's nine-year-old "bad boy" had always given Sheriff Sam Beaudry the perfect excuse to flirt with the pretty single mom…until a child with an incredible secret showed up in town, bringing Sam and Maggie closer than they ever dreamed possible!

#1970 FORTUNE'S WOMAN—RaeAnne Thayne
Fortunes of Texas: Return to Red Rock
P.I. Ross Fortune had his hands full trying to exonerate his sister from a bum murder rap and look after her teenage son in the bargain. Then counselor Julie Osterman stepped up to help, and Ross found himself unable to resist the lovely social worker's appeal.

#1971 A BABY FOR THE BACHELOR—Victoria Pade
Bachelor Noah Perry never expected to meet his mate at a hardware convention; businesswoman Marti Grayson never expected to get pregnant at one! But when they reunited in Northbridge weeks later, they knew something special was building….

#1972 THE MIDWIFE'S GLASS SLIPPER—Karen Rose Smith
The Baby Experts
For Emily Diaz, hiding shameful career secrets from her boss, obstetrician Jared Madison, was bad enough. Falling in love with him as she cared for his twins only made it worse. Would she have her Cinderella moment when all could be forgiven?

#1973 RUNAWAY BRIDE RETURNS!—Christie Ridgway
Injured in a blaze, firefighter Owen Marston got a very special caretaker—runaway bride Izzy Cavaletti, who'd bolted after their quickie Vegas wedding! This time, Izzy realized she couldn't run, let alone hide, from the fire Owen lit in her heart.

#1974 THE DOCTOR'S SURPRISE FAMILY—Mary Forbes
Home to Firewood Island
When her childhood crush, military doctor Dane Rainhart, came home to Firewood Island, it was a dream come true for Kat O'Brien. But could Kat and her little boy be a cure for the heartbreak that ailed the battle-weary M.D.?

SSECNMBPA0409